Letters to Millie

Neal Powers

iUniverse, Inc.
New York   Bloomington

Letters to Millie

Copyright © 2010 by Neal Powers

iUniverse books may be ordered through booksellers or by contacting:
iUniverse
1663 Liberty Drive
Bloomington, IN 47403
www.iuniverse.com
1-800-Authors (1-800-288-4677)

Because of the dynamic nature of the Internet, any Web addresses or links contained in this book may have changed since publication and may no longer be valid. This is a work of fiction. All of the characters, names, incidents, organizations, and dialogue in this novel are either the products of the author's imagination or are used fictitiously.

ISBN: 978-1-4502-3716-1 (pbk)
ISBN: 978-1-4502-3718-5 (ebk)
ISBN: 978-1-4502-3717-8 (hbk)

Library of Congress Control Number: 2010908934

Printed in the United States of America
iUniverse rev. date: 6/18/10

For Mary, Mary, Susan, and Barbara

Acknowledgments

I wish to thank Holly and Van Davis, who have been unwavering in their support. Ted Shank has earned my deep respect for his sacrifice and valor in combat, and for his generous contribution to Raymond's character.

Without encouragement from Mary Stahr, I could not have written a line. She is an oasis of sanity in a crazy world. Narantuya Bayarsaikhan has been a source of great joy in our lives. In Mongolian, her name means "sunshine," and it fits.

The first person to read *Millie's Honor* asked how soon she could read my next novel. Until that moment, I had not considered what would come next. Martha, I hope you and the others who asked for more will not be disappointed.

I am grateful for the help I received from Amber McConkey and Joanne Starer, both gifted editors. Their wisdom and constructive recommendations have certainly improved *Letters to Millie*. Along the way, they helped me become a better writer.

Finally, I am grateful to iUniverse for building creativity into their business model. Thank you.

Prologue

My birth name is Byron Donovan. It says so right on the paper. But everyone around here calls me Brick. It pisses me off. In high school, a hot shot named Raymond Thornton threatened to bash my head in with a brick.

The principal told him, "Thornton, if you brick Donovan, you're out of here."

The name stuck. It's just one reason why I hate him.

I might have turned out better with different parents. I was only eleven when I shot Daddy in the back. He was hitting Mama with an axe handle. I don't even know how many foster homes I was in. I lost track. Mama finally got me back. I think they kept me away from her until Daddy got locked up. Mostly I remember her being drunk.

Folks who knowed Wilmer Donovan called him Butch. I just knowed him as Daddy. He went to prison for trying to kill Mama. They said I saved her life, so they never done nothing to me for it. They just passed me around like a bag of maggots.

Actually, it don't surprise me none that he died inside. A bunch of niggers stabbed him to death in the riot of 61. It just goes to show why I hate them so much.

That's how I got crippled. I was kicking this black kid in the head when Thornton tackled me sideways like. It wasn't no accident. Knees aren't supposed to bend like that. Now my left one don't hardly bend at all. That's the mainest reason he is my enemy. I think about ways to hurt him all the time.

1

I think how much I hate Raymond Thornton every time I pull on a pair of pants or take a crap. Him and his two buddies. Don't matter to me that one of them is the sheriff. They are just a bunch of nigger lovers who ruined my life. I went to prison on account of them. It was bad. There were men there who … well, forget about that.

It's hard to get work after doing time. I drove a garbage truck until they fired me. Today I got like eighty-seven cents to my name. I ain't got nothing more to lose. So my mind is on justice. Just thinking about it makes me feel good.

Daddy did teach me one thing. Revenge is sweet if you can wait for it. Only, strike from behind and use a big stick.

CHAPTER ONE

The Warning

Dutch's Diner, Friday, September 10, 1976

"What in the hell do you mean, you got one too?" Bud Oswald asked.

If it weren't for the sheriff's uniform, he could have passed for a college professor. He wore glasses and had a scholarly look about him.

"Describe it to me in detail. Exactly how did you find it?" he said.

He was speaking to Wally Grayson, a friend he'd known all his life, but at the moment he was in sheriff mode.

Wally stood six two. He was gangly and had shoulders that sloped like a barn roof. He pushed back from the table to put his elbows on his knees. Wally interlaced his fingers and then looked down to concentrate.

"When I came outside this morning to get in the car, a brick was on the hood close to the windshield. It was standing on end in front of the steering wheel," Wally said. He looked up again. "There was no way to miss it."

"Jesus ..." said Raymond Thornton.

Bud shushed him.

"Hold on, Raymond. I'll get back to you in a minute."

He redirected his attention to Wally.

"Which way were the holes facing?"

"Front to rear. I was looking through them when I sat down in the driver's seat."

"What time was this?" Bud asked.

"A little before seven."

Bud turned to look at Raymond. He was slightly built and dressed in jeans and a plaid shirt. He didn't look like a writer. Of course, he didn't look like a war hero, either. Now he built cabinets.

"Okay, Raymond, tell me again."

"Same deal. About seven I came out to get in the pickup, and this brick was standing on my hood, just like Wally said."

"This is bad," said Bud.

"What?" Raymond asked.

"Let's go," the sheriff said. "I've got something to show you."

He placed money on the table and then pushed his chair back. He stood to pull on his leather coat. Raymond and Wally rose, too. Bud reached across the table to collect all three checks.

"I've got this," he said.

Dishes smeared with egg yolks and bacon grease lay scattered around the table. Their coffee had grown cold.

Bud moved fast, his pals right behind him. He handed Dutch Bergen a ten dollar bill.

"Keep the change, Dutch," he said as he headed toward the door.

"See ya, guys," said Dutch.

Raymond and Wally gave him a quick wave as they hurried to keep up with Bud. Outside, the sheriff stopped by the curb. Then he reached into the bed of his pickup truck and held up a brick.

"Did it look like this?" he asked.

"Jesus Christ," Raymond said, nervously chewing a toothpick. "Do you suppose somebody is trying to send us a message?"

"I think we'd better figure out what Brick Donovan is up to," Bud said. "What do you think?"

Wally turned around and propped his rear end against the sheriff's truck. He straightened his tie.

"I'm thinking about Betty Ann and the kids," he said.

"And I'm thinking it's time to mine the perimeter," Raymond said.

"Me too," said Bud.

He ran his fingers through his hair while he analyzed the facts. Something clicked.

"Okay. You guys get in touch with the girls and tell them to be careful. I'm going down to the office to get inside this guy's head. Can we get together tonight?"

"My place?" Wally asked.

"Good."

That was it. They set out in three different directions, each with a purpose.

Bud ran up the steps leading to the sheriff's office. By the time he barged through the door, he was shucking off his coat. Deputy Sam Whiteside looked up to see what all the commotion was about. Without breaking stride, Bud started giving instructions.

"Sam, you're in charge. I want you to run things for a while. I have to figure out what Brick Donovan is up to. Tell dispatch you're handling any sheriff calls today. Use your best judgment, and set aside anything you think I need to see."

He entered his office and hung his coat on the rack in the corner. He walked over to a book shelf and began systematically searching. With a grunt, he took a thick green paperback book down and carried it over to his desk. Glancing up, he noticed several curious faces peering in through the door. Without a word, he walked over to shut it. Then he returned to his desk. Just because he had known Brick Donovan since high school didn't mean he understood him. Now it made a difference.

At Villanova, Bud learned mental illness and criminal behavior were tightly interwoven. He was not a psychologist, but he could read. In front of him lay the *DSM-III*, the third edition of the *Diagnostic and Statistical Manual of Mental Disorders*.

The FBI had profilers. Raleigh County had to settle for Bud Oswald. He wasn't offering counseling. He was trying to understand his clientele from a clinical point of view. It was a more enlightened approach. Otherwise, he would simply beat them into submission like any other cop.

He didn't have time to dig through five hundred pages, so he started with the decision trees near the back of the book. He found the one he wanted on page 345. It covered aggressive and antisocial behavior.

A little over an hour later, Bud sighed and took off his glasses to rub his eyes. He hung one ear piece in his mouth and leaned his chair back to sort out what he had just read. Antisocial Personality Disorder was an adult diagnosis. Conduct Disorder applied to kids under eighteen. From what Bud knew of Brick's childhood, he fit the description of an unsocialized aggressive kid who had made the big time. Donovan was hardwired for violence. Arson was part of the pattern. Compassion was not.

That raised a new question. How extreme was Brick's present crisis? A minute later, he pulled the Raleigh phone book out of his desk. It was less than a half-inch thick. He turned to the yellow pages to find the number for Petiole Hauling. Then he dialed it.

"City Trash. Whatcha want?"

"Melanie, this is Sheriff Bud."

Melanie Griggs weighed about four hundred pounds. Her job title was secretary, but she ran the operation from the front desk.

"Hey, Sheriff. Thanks for calling, but I'm busy tonight."

Bud smiled and shook his head. She was something else.

"Melanie, I need some information. How long has it been since you guys fired Brick?"

"About two months. Why?"

"When did he draw his last paycheck?" Bud asked.

"We paid him cash the day we let him go. Don't want him coming back."

"Has anyone seen him since?"

"Not around here. He didn't exactly make a lot of friends," Melanie replied.

"Okay. That's all I need for now."

Bud swiveled back and forth in his chair and waited. Melanie had a ritual.

"Damn it, Bud. You call and get me all aflutter, and then you hang up on me, just like that?"

Bud waited a decent interval.

"You should know by now, Melanie. That's how I am."

She took a noisy sip of coffee.

"Always breaking my heart. Thanks a lot for calling."

"Hey, you're the one who's busy tonight," Bud said. He was grinning.

This time she made sure the sheriff heard her slurping her coffee.

"Yeah, but you never even asked me to call it off."

Bud chuckled.

"Always good to talk to you, Melanie."

"That does it. Don't ever call me again. We're finished."

"How many times have you said that?"

"Yeah, well this time I mean it. Good-bye."

She hung up on him. Bud laughed out loud. Melanie Griggs had been breaking up with him since first grade. She was getting pretty good at it.

He stood up and stretched before putting his glasses back on. Picking up the *DSM-III*, Bud slipped it back into the gap on the shelf. He pulled his coat off the hook and then opened the door to walk out.

Sam Whiteside looked up from his desk.

"What did you learn?" he asked.

"Brick Donovan is dangerous, desperate, and doesn't know how to back down."

Sam pretended to be in awe.

"Gee, Sheriff. And to think you got all that from a book."

"Don't mess with me, Sam, or you'll get to be boss all weekend."

"Sorry."

Bud started pulling on his coat.

"Look, I've got to go talk to some folks about Brick. If you need, you can call me, but try to keep others from calling. I've got to outthink a nutcase, and I don't have a lot of time. I'll be back this afternoon."

"Got it."

With that, Bud headed for the door. First stop, the Piggly-Wiggly. Raymond was a warrior. Wally was not.

CHAPTER TWO

Precautions

Saturday, September 11, 1976

Indian summer was full of surprises. Today's hot sun beat down on the water, causing Bud to perspire. Of course, being in uniform didn't help. He was on edge. He took off his hat and wiped his brow. The place on his hip where the holster rested was already sticky. He didn't like having to guard Wally Grayson's family.

He kept having a vague notion that he had missed something, but he couldn't identify it. It troubled him. Then he remembered. He hadn't told Tater Gilmore about Brick.

A painter who worked out of Raymond's cabinet shop, Tater was a good man and a good friend. He just happened to be black. Bud made a mental note to contact him as soon as they got off the lake. Bud glanced at Willie Grayson in the bow of the boat. He looked more like Wally every day.

Willie sat up with a start, and the boat rocked gently.

"I got a bite," he said, laughing with excitement.

Bud reached over to get the net in the water.

"Whoa," Willie said, gleefully reeling in the fish. Cautiously he worked it into the net. Bud hauled it out of the water so Willie could see what he caught.

"So, young 'un, what kinda fish have we got here?"

"It's a largemouth," Willie said.

"You know that for a fact, do you?"

"Well, it could be a freak, but I don't think so."

9

"Is it a keeper?" asked Bud.

"Just barely. I say let it go."

Uncle Bud reached into his tackle box. He pulled out a rusty pair of pliers to remove the hook. Once he got it out, he set the fish free.

"Let's go find the ladies and have some lunch."

"Sounds good."

Bud swung around to face the stern and dropped the oars in the water. He was rowing toward shore when Willie asked the question to the back of his head.

"Uncle Bud, I got a question?"

"Go ahead."

"Something's up. You gonna tell me what it is?"

"We're fishing, that's all."

Bud stopped rowing and turned to look at Willie over his shoulder.

Willie nodded his head across the lake, where his mother and his kid sister, Meredith, were fishing from the dock.

"Yeah? So why the badge and gun? Why are Mom and Meredith here?"

Bud let the boat drift. He stared at the dock for a moment. Then he shipped the oars and turned around to face Willie before he answered.

"Well, running a security detail doesn't mean you can't have some fun."

"Security detail? What are you talking about?"

Bud let out a sigh and squinted against the sunlight.

"Something serious has come up. I need your help. We couldn't leave your mom and sister alone today while your dad is at the store."

Willie stared back, eyes wide open. At thirteen, he was sometimes privy to man-talk between his father and his friends. They trusted him. It meant a lot to him.

"Is that what you guys were talking about last night out in the yard?"

"Yes, son, it is. There is a dangerous man on the loose, and he has a grudge against all of us. Thing is, he might be willing to go after anyone in the bunch. So we had to make plans to keep you, your mom, and your sister safe."

"Dangerous how?"

"The guy went to prison for assault. He has a grudge against Uncle Ray. Since I'm the sheriff, he doesn't like me either. This guy is not right in the head. He prefers sneak attacks."

"So how does that involve us?"

"Your dad is a friend. That makes him part of it. I know it sounds crazy, but that's what we're up against. This guy knows we are tight, so he doesn't much care who he attacks. If he hurts one of us, he hurts all of us. We decided it was better to be safe than sorry."

Willie put down his rod. He gripped the seat with both hands, glanced over at the dock, and then and back to Uncle Bud. He had tears in his eyes.

"Looks like that got your attention," Uncle Bud said.

"No foolin'. Shall I just pee in my pants now and get it over with?"

Bud chuckled then shoved his hat back on his head.

"I don't think that will be necessary."

He shifted his weight in the boat.

"Do you remember Brick Donovan?"

"I heard you guys talk about him."

"Okay, well here goes. We think he's the one who burned down Uncle Ray's shop."

"I wondered about that," Willie said.

"The police talked to him, but they couldn't prove anything. A detective over there started sweating him. Then the garbage company fired him. He disappeared for a while, but now we think he's back. That's where you come in."

"Me?"

"Yeah, you."

"In case you hadn't noticed, I'm just a kid."

"Not to me you're not."

"Well, see … I never really got into that whole David and Goliath thing. Besides, Dad doesn't want me going around killing folks."

Bud laughed out loud.

"Fair enough. Here's the deal. Your mom is going to take you and Meredith to Kansas City for a few days. All I want you to do is call me if Brick Donovan shows up there."

Uncle Bud pulled a folded mug shot out of his shirt pocket.

"This is what he looks like. You can't miss him. His left knee is stiff-like."

"So if I call, how long before somebody shows up?"

"Minutes, not hours. I'll call a local sheriff for help. Someone will get there in no time. Can you do that?"

"Yeah, okay. What's the number?"

Bud pulled out a business card. He handed it to Willie.

"Call this number. The dispatchers always know how to reach me. Memorize the number. Okay?"

"Yeah, okay." Willie glanced at the card and then shoved it in his back pocket.

"What's the number?" Bud asked, squinting into the sun.

"Zero two two zero."

"What about the first part?"

"It's easy. Same as everybody else in Raleigh. Nothing to it."

Bud smiled and gave Willie a nod. He was a good kid. Then he turned around to put the oars back in the water. He started rowing to shore again.

CHAPTER THREE

Revenge

Thursday, September 16, 1976

The blue Ford pickup sat behind a row of cedars across the highway from Raymond's shop. Brick saw him arrive a little after seven. He loaded cabinet bases and a countertop in his truck before he drove away. Brick figured that was a good sign. He would be gone awhile.

Brick moistened his lips and wiped his sweaty palms on his jeans. That black painter usually came in around nine. He sometimes wondered if wearing painter's whites made Tater feel whiter. Today he was going to get what he had coming.

Brick ducked down in the seat when he saw his truck pull in. He watched as he loaded plastic buckets of tools in his truck. Then he added a stack of drop cloths. Finally, he put a twelve-foot ladder on top to hold it all down. When Tater climbed behind the wheel without rounding up any buckets of paint, Brick grunted with satisfaction. His plan just might work. He could jump him somewhere between the shop and the paint store.

He waited until Tater got a couple of blocks away before he pulled out onto the highway. By the time they reached the first light, two cars were in between them. When the light changed, Tater made a right turn toward Main Street. Main was a one-way street wide enough for two cars. That meant Brick would have enough room.

The cars ahead went straight through the intersection. At last, it was down to Tater and Brick. He followed at a distance until Tater reached Main. Then he made his move.

13

Brick accelerated hard, pulling up alongside Tater. Then, with his right hand, he hoisted the double-barreled shotgun into the passenger's window and rested it on the window sill. He waited for the black man to look at him. When Tater glanced over, he pulled both triggers.

Brick hadn't counted on the noise. The shotgun blast ruptured his right eardrum. He winced in pain and nearly hit a parked car. The smoking cordite burned his eyes and nose. In the rearview mirror, he watched Tater's truck veer to the right and run up into a yard. Brick slowed down as he approached the city square.

Several blocks ahead, a police car raced across an intersection, lights flashing. Brick couldn't hear the sirens. One block west, a one-way street ran northbound. Brick wondered if they were already responding to a call about the painter.

Timing was everything now. He had created a diversion. Turning left onto Fifth Street, he idled past the county sheriff's office. He double-parked just beyond Bud's truck. When he climbed out, he left the engine running and the driver's door wide open. Brick reached into a cooler and pulled out a bundle of dynamite.

Rounding the back of his truck, he struck a match on the bumper. Then he lit the fuse and rolled the dynamite under Bud's truck. Brick dove behind the steering wheel. He yanked the truck into gear and gunned it, his door slamming shut as he shot forward. Reaching the intersection on a red light, he careened through it anyway, unaware of squealing tires and blaring horns.

Blocks away, a blinding flash lit up his rearview mirrors. Three seconds later the concussion arrived. He felt like a fly slapped with a newspaper. The world went silent. Blood dribbled from his ears. By the time the after-image stopped blooming in his retinas, he was approaching sixty miles per hour. He only had two blocks to slow down. He jammed on the brakes.

Trailing blue smoke, he swerved hard into a left turn. Once he rounded the corner, he forced himself to take a deep breath and slow down. Brick gradually worked his way north. He had one last stop, five blocks away.

He parked his truck in front of Raymond and Millie's house. Again, he left the engine running and the door open. He knew this wouldn't take long. He would be in and out and a hundred miles away before anyone figured out what had happened.

A five-gallon can of gasoline had been careening around in the bed of his truck, sloshing each time it slammed into a wall. It still held about four gallons. Brick went around to the tailgate to retrieve it before he raced for the front door. When he tried the handle, he found it unlocked. The same was true of most homes in Raleigh.

He walked to the far end of the house and entered the kitchen. Sloshing gas in a wide zigzag pattern, he backed through the dining room, taking time to drench the curtains and table cloth. He worked his way out to the entryway. Carefully, he left a clear path to the door. Then he crossed into the living room to soak the couch, chairs, and curtains.

Brick returned to the hall before striking a match and tossing it into the dining room. He watched in fascination as flames rose up before him and began racing toward the kitchen. He crossed over to the living room to toss another lit match. It was a beautiful sight. The burning piano was a nice touch.

Heading toward the front door, he caught movement out of the corner of his eye. He wheeled to see Miss Millie coming down the stairs holding a gun in both hands. Her hair was gloriously red. She was a beautiful. She said something, but Brick couldn't hear her.

"What?" he tried to say, but he didn't know if any sound came out.

She kept coming closer and closer, talking to him, face earnest, the gun aimed at his chest. She looked intense. She was getting too close. He hurled the gas can at her.

In slow motion, he watched her muzzle flash ignite an arc of airborne gasoline. Then something slammed into his chest. It felt like someone hit him with a board. Before he could turn to run, another blow caught him in the throat. The force took him off his feet. He sprawled backward on the floor, stunned and confused. Suddenly, he felt excruciating pain in his legs. He smelled flesh burning. Horrified, he started kicking. When he realized he was on fire, Brick rose to his feet and screamed, bolting for the door. Yet through it all, he heard not a sound.

He fell through the door in a ball of flame, stumbling and then rising, running wildly, trying to escape the pain. He fell again and felt hands grabbing him, slapping his head, his arms, his legs, and rolling him, rolling him, rolling him. Growing faint, he began to tumble end over end through space. Pain engulfed him like a burning sun. At last, he plunged through a sea of fire into a cold blackness beyond.

CHAPTER FOUR

Sheriff's Office

Thursday, September 16, 1976

When Bud heard squealing tires and honking horns, he stood to look out the window. He got no farther than his office door. The explosion overwhelmed his senses: first a thunderclap and then blinding light, searing heat, and a blast wave that hurled him backward. He landed on his butt and slammed into his desk.

He did not see the windows bow in like giant bubbles before bursting into a spray of sparkling shrapnel. He did not see his truck, torn in two, rising past the second-story windows. He was unaware of the burning tires and pieces of truck raining down on the street. His head stopped abruptly when it hit the desk, but his brain didn't. It bounced off the inside of his skull, and his central nervous system shut down.

When he came to his senses, he was lying on the floor in his office near his desk. It was facing the wrong wall. Disoriented, he couldn't figure out where he was. He smelled smoke and felt hot wind blowing through the building. He struggled to his feet, reaching to shove his glasses back up the bridge of his nose, only to find them gone. When he pulled his fingertips away from his face, they were bloody. He fought hard to understand what had just happened.

Staggering out through his office door, he entered a room opened to the outdoors that looked like it had just been ransacked. Everything loose was upended. Papers fluttered in the air. His ears rang, unable to isolate any other sounds. To his left, in the dispatcher's area, he saw Lucy Benedict climbing back onto her chair, searching for her headset.

Whatever had just happened, the epicenter was out in the street. That's where he needed to be. He must take charge of the disaster scene. Bud left bloody smears on the walls as he hobbled down the stairway. In the lobby, the grill of a car poked through the doorway. *It's a Mustang*, he thought, and stored the memory away as though it might be important. He had an incredible headache.

Unable to exit through the front door, he turned toward the emergency door on the side of the building. Then, almost imperceptible to his ringing ears and ruptured eardrums, he thought he heard people calling out.

"God help me," came one cry.

"Oh, sweet Jesus, where am I?" came another.

Sheriff Bud Oswald shoved against the bar on the door and stepped out into daylight. Blood seeped through his uniform. He stepped off into the northbound lane of Business Route 19 and turned slowly to survey the burning, cratered landscape. His legs became rubbery and nausea overtook him. Dropping to his knees, he realized he could still see, but he wasn't sure he wanted to. Then he passed out.

CHAPTER FIVE

Petiole Hauling

Thursday, September 16, 1976

Melanie had grown accustomed to the stench. Just beyond the sagging gates of the landfill, rubbish piled up against the office building. She picked up her yellow mug and savored Jamaica Blue Mountain roast. She always dreamed of traveling the world, but it wasn't possible on her meager salary. Paying for international coffee each month was about as far as her budget would take her.

She put her coffee cup back down in the stains on her desk to fan herself with a paperback book. The cover said "Mickey Spillane" in enormous letters. She was a big fan. Some might even call her a huge fan—just not to her face.

Melanie's phone rang. She snapped her gum and stared at the dial. She had a rule: never answer before the third ring. She wanted people to think she was busy, just like a real office.

"City Trash. Whatcha want?" She didn't mince words.

"Hey, Porky, tell Junior the whole town blew up and I can't finish my route."

Melanie shifted her gum to her cheek and leaned back in her chair in disbelief.

"Kiss my ass, Harlan. What the hell you mean the town blew up? You never used that excuse before."

"Didn't you hear it?"

She picked up the pencil on her desk and twirled it between her fingers.

19

"Naw. I didn't hear nothing. But let's hear the rest of this lie."

"I ain't lying, dammit. It was some kind of bomb. Debris everywhere. I musta picked up scrap iron behind the post office. It got wedged between my tires and poked a hole in both sidewalls. I'm not going anywhere until I get two new tires on the right rear. So, tell Junior if he'd a put a radio in these rigs like we asked, he would be able to figure out where his other haulers are right now."

Melanie scowled. She figured Harlan ruined a couple of tires and was making shit up.

"I ain't delivering no messages for you. You tell him your own self. Hold on." She leaned in to put her elbows on the desk. Melanie wedged the phone into the folds of her sweaty neck as she reached forward to mash a switch on a box in front of her. A buzzer sounded in the next room.

"Dammit, I told you I ain't doin' no business until my head stops hurting," Junior yelled through the door. "So why in the hell are you buzzing me for?"

She picked her gum out of her cheek with two fingers and put it back between her teeth. Then she popped it because it annoyed the hell out of him.

"I adore you, too. It's Harlan. Says the town just blew up. The Packmaster's down, and the other two rigs are God-knows-where. Told me to say, 'I told you so,' about the radios. You gonna take it, or do I gotta call the old man?"

She waited for a three count, knowing she had him.

"Aw, Christ. What next?"

While Junior angrily took the call, Melanie punched up the second line and called her cousin at the tavern. By the time he stormed out of his office, she had more of the story than he did.

Junior was an overweight slob with slicked-back hair and a florid face. His gut drooped over his belt, and his shirttail hung out.

"Holy shit, Melanie! You won't believe what Harlan just tried to tell me."

"Let me guess. Someone shot Tater Gilmore, blew up the sheriff's office, set Millie's house on fire, and Brick Donovan turns up dead in her flower garden. How am I doin'?"

"How the hell do you do that?"

"Do what? I'm just sayin' it's good you fired him instead of makin' him employee of the month. You go find your trucks while I round up two recaps for Harlan."

Junior Petiole swore all the way to his office to get his keys. He swore all the way out the front door. Even after the front door closed, blocking out the sound, Melanie watched him wave his arms and swear all the way to his car.

She propped her chin on her hand and smiled. It was fun to watch Junior fishtail out to the blacktop. She had the best job in the world. They actually paid her to keep him pissed off. Some things mattered more than money.

She shoved aside Mickey Spillane to pull the phone up close.

CHAPTER SIX

Aftershock

Thursday, September 16, 1976

Being idle was not comfortable for Betty Ann. At home there was always plenty of work, but that was the problem. This wasn't her home. It even smelled different. Besides, it felt strange to be here while her brother and his wife were at work. It wasn't her kitchen; it wasn't her laundry room. So aside from letting the dog out every now and then, she didn't even know how to help.

She sat in the living room in a wing-backed chair, legs crossed, balancing a cup of tea on her right knee. The window overlooked traffic on I-70 and an ocean of rooftops across the way. Traffic noise and the buzz of tires on pavement created a droning noise that got on her nerves. So she sipped tea and listened to her children.

Willie was in the family room, playing with his cousin's electric train. Meredith lay sprawled across her bed, reading. Every now and then, she giggled or even laughed out loud. Meredith loved books. She hid flashlights all over her room. When Betty Ann caught her reading under the covers at night, she would take away the flashlight. Meredith would simply go get another one. For now it was okay. Meredith was working on a book report.

A brunette with a wholesome look about her, Betty Ann grew up on a farm doing whatever her brothers did. Often, she did it better. Because of that, she was more at home in the company of men than women.

She took care of herself. Her figure did not reveal that she was the mother of two. In Wally's eyes, she grew more beautiful every day. Others agreed.

Betty Ann missed him. She missed the quiet, and she missed the sounds and smells of her own home. Not knowing how long she would be here made it worse. When the phone rang, she put her cup and saucer on the coffee table and went into the kitchen to answer.

"Betty Ann, I don't have much time, but I couldn't let you find out about it from the radio. Something blew up in downtown Raleigh today," Wally said.

"What happened?"

"I don't know. We were out back unloading the truck. The delivery was late again. The checkout lanes are littered with glass, but we're all okay."

Betty Ann looked puzzled. She started nervously wrapping the telephone cord around an index finger.

"Wait, wait. Wally, say that again. Glass?"

"The windows blew out. Lots of sirens. But we are okay."

She released the cord and touched her forehead with her fingertips.

"I don't understand. What was it? A gas main? Propane truck?"

"I heard all sorts of things between the store and the house," Wally said. "I don't know which ones are true yet. I came home to check the windows and use the phone. All the lines are dead downtown. Power, too. Can you leave the kids at your brother's place? I need help."

Betty Ann hesitated and placed her hand on her hip.

"What kind of help? What haven't you told me?"

Wally paused.

"You sitting down?"

"No. Give me a second."

She stretched the cord across the kitchen and slipped onto the wooden bench of a dinette.

"Okay, now, go."

"Babe, here is what I heard. I don't know any of it for a fact."

Wally hesitated and then told her everything.

"Tater's been shot. Bud is hurt. Ray and Millie's house burned down, and Brick Donovan is lying dead in their front yard."

"What?"

Wally heard the disbelief in her voice, but he continued.

"Lots of folks are injured. Raleigh is like a battle zone right now. I could use a cool head. Can you come?"

"Good Lord!" Betty cried. "Are you serious? Tater … Bud … Millie's house … Did you say Brick is dead?"

"Yep. That's what I've been told."

She started tracing imaginary lines across the table top, trying to connect the dots.

"Wally, give me a second to think. Is this all Brick's doing?"

"That's what folks are saying."

She considered that for a moment.

"So where is Raymond? How is Millie?"

Wally couldn't answer right away. She heard him clear his throat. When he finally spoke, it was in a whisper.

"I don't know. Now you know why I need your help. Fast. I gotta get back to the store to get the windows covered before the place gets looted."

Betty scooted off the bench and stood, hugging herself with her free arm.

"I'll get there as soon as I can."

She started pacing the kitchen, working out a plan in her head.

"I heard traffic's a mess," Wally said. "You may have to park at the football field and hike in. Highway 19 is closed."

She stopped to look out the kitchen window, suddenly aware of the scent of oranges and cinnamon rolls from breakfast.

"Okay. Wally?"

"Yes?"

"Be careful. Don't you get hurt."

"I won't," he said. "But, babe?"

"Yeah?"

"We got some tough days ahead."

"I know. I'm on my way."

CHAPTER SEVEN

The Hospital

Thursday, September 16, 1976

Bud became aware of voices around him. As the darkness receded, he realized someone was speaking to him.

"Sheriff, do you know where you are?'

"I'm not sure," he answered, trying to make out his surroundings. He was lying on a table under a bright light. Many figures stood around him in masks and surgical greens.

"You're at the University Hospital in Claremont. A bomb went off outside your office. You were sprayed with flying glass. We are cleaning you up right now, removing glass and stitching you up."

"My head is pounding."

"You hit your head on something. We sewed up a cut in the back. X-rays didn't show any skull fractures. We had to wait for you to wake up to evaluate you for concussion. Right now we're just glad you're talking to us."

"Can you give me something for the headache?"

"No. Sorry. We need to monitor you. Pain-killers could obscure any problems inside your head."

Bud finally figured out which mask moved when the doctor spoke.

"What about folks in Raleigh? Is anyone hurt? I should be there. I have responsibilities."

Bud felt a gentle hand on his arm.

"This is exactly where you need to be right now. Others have stepped in. We are still picking glass out of you. We're only halfway through. I'm Dr. Steadman, and my colleague over there is Dr. Winthrop. He's taking one side and I'm taking the other. We'll get you out of here as soon as we can."

Another voice spoke, this time from Bud's left.

"Sheriff, you're a very lucky man."

"Oh really? What makes you say that?"

"Your glasses saved your eyes."

"How do you know I wear glasses?"

"When your look in the mirror, you'll see."

The first voice spoke again.

"We'll help you relax a little bit so we can finish up. It won't take long now."

Three hours later, nurses wheeled Bud out of the operating room. Wally was waiting for him. He walked beside the gurney as they took him to the recovery room. Wally stood out in the hall until the nurses finished. He stepped into the room when they could be alone. Then he told the sheriff what he knew. Tears flowed down Bud's cheeks, stinging his lacerated face. Wally placed a hand on Bud's forearm.

"We can sort all this out later. Right now we need you back on your feet. Sam will take care of things until you get out of here. For now, heal up and get some rest. You're going to need it."

"Sounds like it," Bud said. He was getting drowsy. They must have given him something. He dozed off.

CHAPTER EIGHT

Brick Donovan's Trail

Friday, September 17, 1976

Bud's head hurt, and he didn't recognize his surroundings. Then he remembered. He was in the hospital. He put a hand to his face. It was painful, like a bad sunburn. His face was covered with tiny bumps, and he had sutures here and there. Craning his neck to find a mirror, he noticed a figure sitting next to the bed. He really needed his glasses.

"Morning, Sheriff. Glad to see you stirring."

Bud recognized the voice.

"Hey, Sam, what time is it?" he asked.

"It's a little after six. I thought I'd check with you before morning roll call."

Bud pulled himself up and tried to clear his head.

"Sam, can you crank this bed up?"

Sam stood up and stabbed at a button or two until he found the right one.

"Say when."

"There. That's good." Bud cleared his throat.

"Okay, Sam, bring me up to speed."

About the time Sam finished, a nurse barged in with a bedpan.

"Sheriff, would you mind? I need to measure your output."

"What's your name?"

"Lillian."

"Lillian, I thank you for all you have done. But I have to get out of here. Please pull this IV and help me find my clothes."

"Sheriff Oswald, you really should stay here for another day or so."

"I don't doubt that for a minute. Now where are my pants?"

Bud swung his legs off the edge of the bed and shifted forward to stand.

Lillian hesitated at the foot of the bed and looked at Deputy Whiteside for support. He wasn't much help. He folded his arms and gave her a little shrug. Bud reached over to start peeling away the surgical tape on the back of his hand before she finally moved.

"Okay, okay, okay."

She stepped in and pulled the needle out.

"Sheriff," she said, "your shirt was ruined. Take the gown home with you."

She reached under the bed and pulled out his pants.

"These aren't much better. Can you dress yourself?"

"After all these years, I think so."

He was pretty unsteady.

"Thank you, Lillian. If I didn't have to protect the folks in Raleigh County, I would stay longer. As it is, Sam and I have a lot of work to do."

"I understand. Just do a favor for me, will you?"

"What's that?"

"Work from home for a couple of days. You lost quite a bit of blood. There's something else you should know."

"Can you tell me, or do I have to figure it out for myself?" Bud asked.

"It is impossible for the doctors to get all the glass. Slivers may keep working to the surface for a long time. You'll get most of them in a few weeks, but don't be surprised years from now if you find another when you're shaving."

Bud considered what she just said.

"That's good to know," he said.

Bud looked over at Sam for a moment.

"Warn the deputies that I will be somewhat prickly," he said.

He fished one foot into his slacks. Then he shifted his weight and started with the other foot. Sam reached out to steady him.

"No need, Sheriff. They've all figured it out by now."

Bud pulled his pants up underneath the hospital gown and then zipped them up and fastened his belt. He nodded to Lillian.

"How do I look?" he asked.

"Do you really want to know?"

"Probably not. Give the doctors my regards," he said. "Now, where are my shoes?"

Sam drove the cruiser up to the portico where Bud sat in a wheelchair.

"Hospital rules," Nurse Lillian had said.

After Bud eased into the passenger seat, Sam hesitated.

"Where to, Sheriff?"

"The office, please."

"Bud, you look like hell. Are you sure you want to do this?"

"No, Sam, I don't. But I figure folks there will understand if I am out of uniform. What do you think?"

"Tell you what. Let's swing by your house so you can change," Sam said. "I can take you back home later."

"That's a deal. I need a damage assessment and a timeline on Brick's movements. Think that's possible?"

"Yes, sir. We're already working on it."

They drove in silence for a moment, until Sam cleared his throat.

"You got something to say, Sam?"

"Yes, sir."

"Well, go ahead."

Sam glanced over at Bud briefly.

"Did you hear about Lucy?" he asked.

"No."

"She really held the department together. It was remarkable. She commandeered a couple of walkie-talkies and got everybody rolling. It was over an hour before we realized she was hurt."

"What?"

The memory came back like a snapshot. When Bud had stumbled for the stairway, he saw her returning to the console.

"Her back was toward the window," Sam said. "Her head and shoulders caught a lot of glass, but she didn't let on. She got things launched using a pair of handhelds."

Bud rubbed his hand through his hair and turned to look out the window.

"Where is she now? Is she going to be all right?"

"Doctors seem to think so. She was just a few doors down the hall from you. She is one tough cookie. She saved a lot of lives yesterday."

"Sam, get the details to me as soon as you can. We can't let that go unnoticed."

Instead of going home after roll call, Bud ended up in the back room at Dutch's Diner. His office was in shambles, his head was pounding, and he needed coffee. He saw no purpose in alarming the patrons. For that matter, Dutch himself wouldn't maintain eye contact for long, so he didn't hesitate when Sheriff Bud said he needed to read something without interruption.

Preliminary Timeline, September 16, 1976
(Brick Donovan)

Approx. 9:15 AM – Resident in yard at Ninth and
Main hears racing engines, sees two trucks
"drag-racing" down Main Street. When they get
approx. one half block south, witness sees smoke,
hears loud boom. The truck on the right veers
into a yard and strikes a neighbor's porch. The

31

*other truck, described as greenish-blue, speeds
away. Witness calls police.*

*9:21:32 AM – Raleigh Police Department dispatchers
receive multiple calls about a car wreck in the
seven hundred block of Main St. Raleigh PD
Unit 3 takes call.*

*9:24:42 AM – RPD Unit 3 reaches accident site at 715
North Main, reports a black male is seriously
injured, requests ambulance.*

*9:25:29 AM – Raleigh Police Department relays
ambulance request.*

*9:25:56 AM – Raleigh County Ambulance District
dispatches unit to the scene. They transport.
Victim pronounced DOA at Raleigh County
Hospital.*

*Approx. 9:26 AM – A pedestrian crossing Main at Fifth
St. sees blue pickup double-park. Bearded white
male exits vehicle, leaves door open, blocks eastbound traffic. Witness sees driver pull package
out of truck, walk around behind vehicle. Driver
tosses object under vehicle at curb. Driver returns
to truck, speeds away. Witness states, "When I
seen him lay rubber, I knew something bad was
coming." The witness entered the bank moments
before explosion. Multiple witnesses report blue
pickup running red light at Fifth and Highway
19, speeding eastbound.*

*9:27:42 AM – Explosion occurs outside county office
building.*

*9:29:13 AM – Sheriff Dept. dispatcher calls hospital,
requests all available ambulances to her location,
activates disaster plan.*

*Approx. 9:32:00 AM – All Sheriff Department
communications down due to fire.*

*9:35:29 AM – Det. Shoemaker, Raleigh Police
Department, calls city dispatch, requests ID
of shooting victim. He diverts to Biederman
Cabinetry to look for Raymond Thornton.*

*9:38:11 AM – RPD Unit 3 relays identity of victim,
Lucius "Tater" Gilmore. Det. Shoemaker names
possible perp as Brick Donovan.*

*9:41:07 AM – Sheriff dispatcher establishes two-way
radio contact with Raleigh Police Department.
Coordinated disaster response begins.*

*9:46:44 AM – Shoemaker clears cabinet shop enroute to
disaster scene.*

*9:52:24 AM – Shoemaker reports column of smoke
northeast of downtown. Requests fire department
to area of Civic Park. No units available.*

*9:58:08 AM – Shoemaker reports fire at 914 East Tenth,
man down.*

*10:08:55 AM – Fire unit responds. One deceased, one
injured, property destroyed. Blue 1972 Ford
pickup idling at curb, driver's door open, shotgun
lying on seat.*

*10:23:45 AM – Det. Shoemaker transported to hospital,
second and third degree burns.*

*1:30 PM – Arson unit detects accelerant. Unidentified
victim found in house. Victim is deceased.
Raleigh Police Department crime unit finds
gunpowder residue inside truck cab, shotgun
recently fired, two empty cartridges chambered.
Vehicle registered to Byron Donovan, who had
been found deceased at the scene due to severe
burns and multiple gunshot wounds.*

*Note: Greenlee Refractory conducted an inventory
following the explosion in Raleigh. They reported*

*a break-in at Mine No. 6 sometime within the
past week. A padlock on one of their trailers
had been cut with bolt-cutters. Several sticks of
dynamite and two fused primers were missing.*

CHAPTER NINE

The Opportunist

Friday September 17, 1976

Raleigh Journal-Messenger

Local Man Leaves Trail of Death, Mayhem
Three dead, 21 hurt

By Lou Baxter, Editor

> *It will take many years for Raleigh to get over what took place here yesterday. Our community lost three citizens in what seems to be a homicide, an act of arson, and a shooting in self-defense. Dead are Mrs. Margaret Millicent (McKenna) Thornton, age 43, a beloved high school English teacher, Lucius "Tater" Gilmore, age 29, a local businessman and friend of Mr. and Mrs. Raymond "Sonny" Thornton, and the man thought responsible for their deaths and injuring twenty-one others with an explosive device, Byron "Brick" Donovan, age 34.*

Garrett Stilton studied the newspaper article in his shabby legal office above the drug store. There had to be an angle. He worried about it long into the night. A few years back, Brick Donovan was charged with aggravated assault. Garrett Stilton was appointed his public defender.

Since an entire Physical Education class witnessed the attack, there hadn't been much room for a defense. Stilton needed the money, so he convinced Brick he got him a light sentence. That was easy for him to say. He wasn't a twenty-year-old kid about to do time in the Missouri State Penitentiary.

He still needed money, so not that much had changed in his life—except for the divorce. But Stilton could smell opportunity. He needed to find an angle.

He wore ill-fitting suits because he was shaped like a football. His head was small, and the way he combed his hair back only drew attention to it. He had multiple chins and an exaggerated spare tire. Below, his legs tapered to tiny feet. Exercise was out of the question.

When Stilton was still a teenager, he made a huge mistake. While building a float for a parade, a neighbor kid had hitched a flat-bed trailer to his truck and driven off with a load of teenagers. Instead of hanging on for dear life, Stilton decided to show off. He stepped over the front bar and stood on the hitch. It was a stupid thing to do. Jumping off was even worse. A piece of angle iron sliced across the back of his leg and severed his Achilles tendon. Today he still lurched along with a floppy foot. Folks in town called him Tiltin' Stilton, and it made him furious.

Right now he was thinking about what two people trapped inside a burning building might do. He finally saw an opening. It would work if he could convince a jury that it didn't really matter how the fire started. Wouldn't a reasonable man expect two victims trapped in a fire to work together to escape? Instead, Millie Thornton shot Brick with a high-caliber handgun. If that wasn't attempted homicide, it was at least criminal negligence—manslaughter. There might be a lawsuit hiding in there somewhere.

That was when he saw his angle. He might be able to make a wrongful death lawsuit stick. He put the newspaper aside and pulled out the *Missouri Statutes*. Soon he was reading what the state had to say about wrongful deaths.

His chair squeaked when he tilted back. It needed oil. But if it came down to deciding whether to buy oil or a hamburger, he could live with a squeaky chair. In fact, that was the problem he was trying to solve. Before long, he devised a scheme.

If Brick Donovan's mother was still alive and able to sign her name, he could represent her in a suit against Millie's estate and pick the Thorntons clean. The last time he saw Mama, she was drinking like a professional. He prayed he could find her before her liver failed. She might go for it if he waved a little money in front of her.

With very few facts to guide him, he began drafting two documents. The first was a letter to Raymond "Sonny" Thornton claiming one and a half million dollars in damages. The second was a filing for a wrongful death lawsuit.

It took him a few days, but he found Brick's mother watching soap operas in a state institution. He sent the letter to Raymond by certified mail, return receipt requested. He hoped for a quick settlement. He needed to cash in before his client expired. He always did his best work outside the courtroom.

CHAPTER TEN

Strong Women

Saturday, September 18, 1976

For some reason, Betty Ann expected the morgue to have gray walls. These were light yellow, almost cheery. She expected some kind of viewing window. Instead, the detective from Raleigh and a guy in a lab coat escorted her through double doors. They entered a room with a wall of stainless steel lockers. She wondered how they kept the bodies cold. She remembered the meat locker in town. There, everything was covered with frost. Here there was no frost. How did they do that? It didn't smell the same, either.

Where's all the refrigeration equipment? Maybe it is on the roof. That's where a lot of air conditioning units go. She imagined they were heavy. *How would you design a building to carry the extra load?*

Betty Ann managed difficult times by focusing on minute details. It was her way of avoiding the really big things as long as she could. But now she was running out of time.

"No hurry. Just tell me when you're ready," the attendant said.

She decided this had to be the worst part of his job. She took a deep breath and looked around at her surroundings. She was about to see the charred remains of their laughing, joyous Millie.

War hero or not, Betty Ann knew that Raymond could not handle it. His last vision of Millie should not be on a stainless steel tray. She hugged herself tightly and nodded to the attendant.

"Let's get this over with," she said.

She would always regret it. Intellectually, she knew that she was not looking at Millie. It was only her chrysalis. But it was the most horrifying thing she had ever seen. Still, if it came down to it, she would do it again to spare Raymond.

There wasn't much to go on except for a swatch of red hair and Millie's personal effects. She recognized the watch and wedding band.

On the way home, detective Bob Kuhlmann began prattling about a Smith and Wesson found on the floor beside Millie's remains. Betty Ann stared out the window, barely listening.

"In a revolver," he said, "the bullets go in the cylinder. This one won't rotate any more. Some of the bullets exploded during the fire and split it open," he said.

"Why are you telling me this?" Betty Ann asked. She looked down at her folded hands. It was the only way she could control the trembling.

He ignored her question for the moment.

"Did you ever notice the little silver button in the bottom of a bullet?" he asked.

"I guess so. Why?"

"That's the primer. Fulminate of mercury. When the hammer strikes, it fires sparks through a hole into the gunpowder. When you think about it, it's not much different than lighting the fuse on an old-time cannon."

Betty Ann turned to look at him carefully.

"That brings me back to my question. Are you trying to tell me something?" she asked.

He paused. Then he explained.

"There were no primers in the four rounds that blew up. The explosions popped them out of the casing. Two rounds still had primers in them. They both had a dimple from the hammer," he said.

"Are you saying Millie fired two shots?"

He briefly glanced over at her. She was paying attention now. He started to drum his fingers on the steering wheel.

"Yes. But there is more to it than that."

39

He cleared his throat before he continued.

"Brick was something like eighteen feet away. At that distance, a lot of shots go wild, but not Millie's. Two shots. Two hits …"

His voice trailed off until it was almost a whisper.

"It was like she knew what she was doing."

Betty Ann thought about that in silence. When she finally spoke, her voice was thick. Tears ran down her cheeks.

"Will you do me a favor?" she asked.

"Sure."

"Will you tell Raymond? He needs to know."

The cop twisted his neck until it cracked. Then he swallowed hard.

"Sure thing," he said.

They finished the drive in silence.

Sitting now in her own kitchen, Betty Ann stared into a cup of tea while she forced herself to compartmentalize her memories of the visit to the coroner's office. She could always grieve about that later. Right now she was thinking about Raymond and his Vietnam buddies.

Three pals escaped Vietnam together and bought Harleys in Seattle to ride back to the Midwest. They went first to Indiana to drop off the Hoosier, and then to Asheville where the second one lived. Finally, Raymond headed back to Raleigh alone.

Within six months, both of his buddies had committed suicide, one in a barn with a shotgun, the other inside a running car in a closed garage. Betty Ann could see Millie's death driving Raymond over the edge. The hair stood up on the back of her neck when she thought about it. What could she do? She walked to the wall phone and lifted the handset off the hook.

"Sheriff's department. How may we help you?" said a pleasant professional voice.

"This is Betty Ann Grayson. Is Sheriff Oswald back in the saddle? I'd like to talk to him, please."

"Is he expecting your call?"

40

Betty Ann recognized the voice now.

"Is this Elaine?" she asked softly.

"Yes, it is."

"Elaine, I don't know how to tell you how sorry I am about Tater. We loved him."

"Thank you, Mrs. Grayson. I do appreciate that."

Betty Ann stood with one hand to her forehead, praying. There was a long silence before Elaine resumed. Her voice quavered.

"Let me put you through."

Betty waited for the call to be transferred. She knew Elaine would tell Bud who was calling.

"Oswald," came the answer.

"Grayson," said Betty Ann in her deepest voice.

"Okay, Betty Ann. Sorry. I'm up to my elbows trying to get the department put back together. What can I do for you?" Bud said.

"Where is Raymond?" she asked.

"He's in the back. Local cops found him passed out in his truck last night. They had the decency to deliver him to the Raleigh County home for wayward heroes," Bud answered.

"Do you think he would be willing to come stay here for a while? We can put him up in Willie's room."

Bud considered it.

"I'll make it a condition for his release. How's that?"

"We'll be ready tonight," Betty Ann said.

"I'll bring him over myself."

"Thanks, Bud. I'll let you get back to what you were doing."

Before Bud dropped Raymond off, Betty Ann tried to prepare the kids. She talked to them during dinner.

"Uncle Ray lost Aunt Millie," she told them. "He is heartsick and lonely. He needs family, and we're all he has. That's where you two come in."

She piled pork chops and mashed potatoes on their plates and started adding gravy.

"How, Mama?" Willie asked.

She stopped to look at him. This was important.

"When he got back from the war, he would get drunk just to block the grief. We may not be able to stop him from doing it again. But we can keep him safe and give him time to heal. Next to Millie, you kids mean more to him than anybody. So love him. Stay with him. Give him reasons to live. Otherwise, he might go looking for Millie and never come back."

She spooned fruit salad onto both plates.

"You mean, like … like … kill himself?" Willie asked.

She stopped, spoon hovering in midair.

"Yes. Raymond has seen too much death. He can't stand to lose anyone else. Problem is, life comes with losses. So we need to love Raymond all we can. Just don't let him know why we are doing it."

Meredith looked at her mama with big eyes.

Try as hard as she might, Betty Ann could not talk Raymond out of sleeping on the couch. When she pressed him, he finally told her why.

"I have night terrors. If I am upstairs, I will wake the whole household. You folks don't need that. If I am on the couch, I can just go stand on the porch until I calm down. That will actually be better for me."

She put a hand on his arm and looked at him tenderly.

"Okay," she said. "Just remember that you are here because we love you."

His eyes brimmed with tears, but his voice failed him. Raymond nodded his head and wept. Betty Ann left him alone, sitting on the couch with a pile of sheets and blankets. As she started up the stairs, she realized she was bone weary.

In the darkened bedroom, she stripped down to her panties and pulled on a flannel nightgown. When she lifted the covers and slid into bed, Wally reached for her. He held her close and scooted up behind her. He kissed her on the ear.

"You're safe now. I've got you," Wally whispered.

Feeling his warmth against her, Betty clutched her pillow to her face and sobbed. Wally held her tightly and let her cry.

On the morning of Millie's funeral, Betty Ann entered the kitchen just as Meredith crawled up on the couch to sit on top of Raymond. The little girl flung her arms around his neck and began weeping big wet tears onto his chest.

Betty Ann headed for the living room to stop her, but it was too late. Raymond was awake.

"Whoa, sunshine," he said. "What is it? You thinking about Aunt Millie?"

Meredith nodded her head between her arms and began to sob.

Betty Ann hovered in the doorway, uncertain what to do next.

"Me, too, honey, me, too." He wept with her.

Betty froze. She decided to let this play out. After a moment, Meredith rose up on her elbows to look at him.

"Don't go, Uncle Ray. Please don't go."

"What do you mean, Meredith? Sooner or later I have to leave."

"Nooooo!" howled Meredith.

"Sweetie, I can't stay here forever. This is your living room. Sooner or later you need to have it back," Raymond said.

"That's not what I mean, Uncle Ray. I just don't want to not never see you again, like Aunt Millie."

Betty Ann covered her face with her hands and withdrew into the kitchen. She left the door open so she could listen.

"Meredith, I don't understand."

"Mama told us to stick by you. To make sure you didn't miss Aunt Millie so much that you want to die to be with her. She said hang on to you and don't never let go. She told us don't tell you, but I just can't."

Betty Ann wheeled in disbelief.

She saw Raymond roll onto his back, sobbing uncontrollably, cradling Meredith in his arms, stroking her hair, kissing the top of her head. Raymond tried several times to speak, but his voice kept choking up. Betty Ann's eyes flooded with tears. Finally, she heard Raymond whisper.

"Okay," he said. "I promise. I won't go looking for Aunt Millie. I'll stay here with you awhile longer. But neither one of us has to tell your mommy. Okay?"

Betty Ann sat down on a kitchen chair. She swallowed quietly.

"God bless that child," she thought. "She got through to him when none of the rest of us knew how."

Tears ran down her jaw line and plunged down her neck. She wiped them away, stood up, tightened her robe, and got busy in the kitchen. It was time to wake the household with the smells of coffee, bacon, and biscuits.

CHAPTER ELEVEN

Lucy

Tuesday, September 21, 1976

Lucy rapidly grew tired of lying on her stomach. She improvised a way to prop herself up so that her back and shoulders did not rub against the bedding. Even that grew tiring after a while, so she shifted into one of the chairs. First she draped a blanket across the back. Then she eased back on it very slowly and did not move.

That's what she was doing when Sheriff Bud Oswald appeared to look in on her. His face looked like her shoulders felt. He sat down in the opposite chair and asked her about her wounds. He listened intently while she answered. Then he asked her to describe what happened after the bombing. Not once did he interrupt.

"Remarkable," he said when she finished. Then he leaned back in his chair and studied her for a few moments.

"You are very brave. No telling how many lives you saved that day. I admire you for your commitment."

No one had ever spoken that directly with her before. She just thought she was doing her duty. In the bright light of Bud's attention, she blushed. She didn't do that often. It did not pass unnoticed.

Lucy laughed nervously and tossed around her half a head of hair. The back of her head had been shaven.

"What do you think I should do about this?" she asked, pulling out some of the remaining strands of hair.

"Probably what I will have to do about this," Bud said, touching his growth of beard. "We'll just have to figure out how to leave it alone until we heal up. What do you think?"

"I'm thinking about having the rest of it shaved off and wearing a wig for a while."

"That's very practical. Sort of a radical way to get there, but short hair might be very becoming. Guess you get to find out, one way or the other," Bud said. His eyes were smiling, but otherwise he maintained a professional demeanor. She spotted the incongruity, and read it correctly. The sheriff was definitely interested. She made a mental note.

Lucy Benedict also noticed a difference when she returned to work. Others treated her with heightened respect. And, unless she was mistaken, the sheriff's gaze seemed to dwell on her longer than she recalled. Because he treated her respectfully, eye contact with Bud made her tingle. It was a pleasant feeling. She just wasn't sure whether she was ready to cross the minefield known as an office romance. She decided to be patient. If it was meant to be, it would happen.

CHAPTER TWELVE

Settling Accounts

Thursday, September 23, 1976

Raymond stood in the gravel driveway beside the lawn jockey. The small bowlegged figure held a rusty iron ring up in his right hand. His coat was fire-engine red and his face painted white. It was Julius' little joke. He installed it in 1958 when Raleigh High School finally integrated. Now it was a point of community pride. Raymond reached out to touch the place on the jockey's cap where so many fingers had rubbed through the paint.

He sighed, and thought about two dead Gilmores: Larry, killed accidentally during Vietnam, and Tater, shot dead just days ago. Julius was uncle to the first and father to the second. Raymond dreaded seeing Julius and Elaine Gilmore, but Raleigh was too small. Sooner or later they would meet.

The screen door swung out, ringing musically as its spring sawed into the wood.

"Raymond Thornton, is that you? Get yourself on in here, son. I been expecting you."

Julius had white hair, a white cane, and empty eyes. He cocked his head to listen. Raymond took a deep breath.

"Mr. Gilmore, how did you know it was me?"

"Well, now, just how many motor-sickles in Raleigh are gonna pull up in front of my house?"

"Good point," Raymond answered. He hesitated. "Sir, I came to tell you how sorry I am about Tater. I feel bad that I wasn't at the funeral."

"Don't know why you should. Had two funerals the same day, one of them your wife. I knowed where you was."

Mr. Gilmore held the door open and stood to the side.

"You were a good friend, but a man can only handle so many funerals in one day. So come on in and sit awhile. It'd be a comfort to me."

Raymond walked up the drive to the porch.

"Thank you, sir. I'd like that."

The last time Raymond had been in the Gilmores' home, he told stories about Chicago. He and Bud, encouraged by Larry, Julius' nephew, had broken curfew to tour the jazz clubs after-hours. The highlight of their mischief was listening to a jam session with Miles Davis. Larry's loss still hurt as much as Tater's.

Raymond thought of Julius as a wise man. He had a nose for guilt. Surely he understood that crazy folks could hurt innocent people.

Raymond was right. In his gentle way, Julius began easing the burden of Tater's death from Raymond's shoulders. Even Elaine Gilmore, a gracious hostess, made him feel welcome. It was hard because Raymond felt that Tater was dead because of him.

When night fell, Raymond's Harley stood on its kickstand in the driveway. He had accepted their invitation to stay for pot roast, stewed potatoes and carrots, and the best cherry pie in town.

Raymond was astonished when Elaine hugged him before he left. She insisted he come see them again. Raymond promised.

Raymond overheard their conversation as he left, but he gave no indication.

"Do you think that man is gonna be all right?" Elaine asked softly as Raymond walked down the driveway, pulling on leather gloves.

"About as well as a man can be who lost his wife and a good friend on the same day," Julius answered. "You were kind to him, Elaine, and

I thank you for that. If he comes back, it will be on account of your pot roast."

Raymond's eyes filled with tears. He fought hard not to sob out loud. He heard them turn and go inside. Raymond swung his leg over the Harley then looked down to say a silent prayer for Tater and Larry. Then he thumbed the starter.

The engine fired up with a belch. He made a wide U-turn in front of the Gilmores' house and headed back to town. At the stop sign, he turned left onto McAlister. Two blocks later, he realized he was heading to a home that no longer existed. Nothing waited for him there but a black hole in the ground.

He sat at the intersection for a moment, bike propped up between outstretched legs. He listened to the staggered idle of the Harley. If it were not for Betty Ann and the kids, he would go to a liquor store.

He turned down Main Street. Perhaps he could see Meredith and Willie before they went to bed. He shifted up through the gears. The signs said 20 mph, but experience had taught him that the cobblestone ride smoothed out at forty-eight.

He knew the cops wouldn't like what he was about to do. He needed to get to the bottom of Main Street before they got here, so he dialed in more throttle. Flying down the hill toward the ball field, Raymond downshifted noisily and nursed the brakes to slow below 20 mph before swinging out onto the highway. He waved at the cruiser when it roared past in the opposite direction.

If he didn't cool it, the cops were going to stop snoozing behind the bowling alley. He watched for the black-and-white's next move in his rearview mirrors. The cruiser pitched into the entrance of the drive-through bank and then spun a tight 180 and zoomed back uphill after the Harley.

Raymond waved a second time from the parking lot of the Dog'n'Suds. In the minute it took for the officer to crank it around again and pull into the parking lot, Raymond had the bike on the kickstand and his helmet off. He mashed the button on the squawk box and placed his order.

Officer Crocker pulled up behind the bike and leaned out of his window.

"Thornton, what in the hell do you think you are doing?"

Raymond smiled innocently.

"Getting you a root beer float, officer. Why? What did you think I was doing?"

"Dammit, Ray. You can't keep ripping up and down Main Street on that thing. Someone is gonna get hurt."

Raymond looked confused and then took a step toward the highway to point out where he had seen the patrol car speeding by.

"You know, Lee, I was just thinking the same thing watching you race up and down Mallinckrodt Hill in the dead of night."

He turned and shrugged, both palms upward.

"Of course, there is a difference between you and me."

"You're damn right, there is. I've got a job to do," Officer Crocker scowled.

Raymond folded his arms.

"That wasn't what I had in mind."

"Oh really? So what's the difference?"

The carhop came out with two mugs on a tray. Raymond paid her and then walked over to the police cruiser with the tray, and smiled.

"Simple. I saw you. You didn't see me. Would you like a root beer float?"

The next day, Raymond went after the information he needed. He rode into the university hospital parking lot and found a parking place. He rode past it and then put the bike in neutral and backed it in against the curb. Pulling out straight ahead would be easier and safer when he decided it was time to leave.

Inside the lobby, he noticed the hospital smells. It didn't bother him. He had smelled things a lot worse. He asked at the information desk about Detective Ned Shoemaker, saying that he was a close personal friend. He was given the room number and the directions to the elevator.

On the seventh floor, he reported to the nurse's station and identified himself. They directed him to the room.

According to the *Journal-Messenger*, it was an undisclosed location. So much for that.

He walked in and stood silently until Shoemaker realized there was someone standing in the door.

"How did you find me?" Shoemaker asked.

"Paper said you had second- and third-degree burns. Around here, that means this place. Where else would they take you?" Raymond answered.

"How did you know I wasn't at the Mayo Clinic?"

"On the department's budget? Come on, Ned. Give me some credit."

Raymond took in the bandages on Ned's hands and forearms, and noticed another on his scalp. Ned had really offered himself up to save Brick.

"Okay. You found me. So did you come to finish me off or what?"

Raymond hovered near the door. He didn't know what to say next. Tears trailed from Shoemaker's eyes. Raymond knew the overwhelming guilt that comes when someone dies on your watch. It happened to him too often in Vietnam.

"Ned, I came here hoping we could both find a little peace," said Raymond in a husky voice. Then he shifted off the door frame and entered the room.

Shoemaker turned his face away to look out the window. It was night outside, but it was better than looking Millie's husband in the eye.

"I'm fresh out of that. I keep thinking Millie is dead on account of me."

Raymond let out a sigh. He walked across the room to the chair by the window. He sat down to lower his eye level. In the process, he made eye contact with Ned.

"I thought so. For cops, things have to be black and white," Raymond said. "But Millie's death has a whole lot of gray. Besides,

Ned, it's just as much my fault as yours. I'm the one Brick was really after."

Raymond pressed his right fist into his left palm. "Millie just put a stop to it. The truth is, you didn't have enough time."

A long silence occurred as Ned considered that.

Raymond folded his arms, tucking his hands into his armpits. He waited. Finally, Ned spoke.

"I was five minutes too late, Ray."

Raymond closed his eyes and wished it were otherwise. But in every after-action report, his buddies always second-guessed themselves.

"But you were the only one who figured it out. You got there. Look at me. I was in the next county over. Brick Donovan is the one who killed Millie, not you."

Raymond looked out the window to allow Ned time to process that notion. It was not right to hate this guy, he thought over and over.

A long silence passed. Finally, when Ned spoke, his voice was raspy.

"But if I had let him burn, maybe I could have gotten her out."

Raymond looked at him again. He leaned back in the chair and rubbed his forehead with the heal of one hand.

"Quit punishing yourself for stuff you didn't know."

"What are you getting at?"

Raymond lowered his hand and sat forward to look Ned in the eye.

"What choice did you have, Ned?" he said, pointing to an imaginary man on the floor. "Step over a burning man and say, 'Excuse me, I ought to go ring the doorbell. See if anybody is home?'"

Ned squirmed in the bed and took in a ragged breath.

"Maybe you're right," he said. "But I still feel like I helped the wrong one."

Raymond rose and stepped closer to the bed, placing a hand on the detective's shoulder. He leaned down close to Ned's ear and spoke softly.

"That's my point. You can say that now because you know how it turned out. But at the time you didn't know Millie was home, did you?"

"No," Ned said, shaking his head.

"Of course not," Raymond said. "Everyone in town expected her to be at school, even Brick."

He glanced down for a moment, and then made eye contact with Ned.

"What you did was try to save a man who was dying right in front of you. That is no cowardly act."

A long, awkward pause passed between them. Ned's closed his eyes, but he saw visions of Brick on fire, so he opened them and looked away. He swallowed hard.

"So how bad are the burns?" Raymond asked.

"Second degree, mostly." Ned moved his arms clumsily. "The worst is where my coat sleeve melted on my arm. I still have ten fingers. I just don't know how well they'll work."

Raymond sat down and propped his elbows against his knees. He leaned in toward Shoemaker.

"I'm praying you heal up good as new," Raymond said.

He glanced at the floor, and accepted the notion there was no easy way.

"Listen, Ned, I need something from you."

Ned looked apprehensive.

"What's that?"

"I need to know what Millie went through. Did Brick say anything that'd help me put her to rest?"

Raymond leaned back in the chair and tried to act calm.

"He was in a lot of pain, and losing blood fast. Rolling him and putting out the fire, there was so much blood. On him. On me. On the grass. That's how I knew he'd been shot. I heard muffled pops, more like firecrackers. I pulled my weapon and headed for the house, but the heat was too intense. I never even got to the porch. Fire was rolling out through the front door and windows."

Raymond tapped his fingertips together.

"What happened to Millie? What did you hear? Did she … suffer?"

Ned hesitated.

"That was the spooky part."

"What?"

"Brick was yelling and carrying on, but from the house all I heard was fire. No cries. Just burning. I puked in the grass. By the time the medics got to me, I was out of my head. They said it was the burns. They gave me morphine and I didn't care anymore. I just wanted to go away."

They both sat in silence for a moment.

"And now?" Raymond asked

Ned shot an angry glance at him.

"And now, what?"

"With what you know now, how do you figure it? The chain of events. What happened to Millie?"

"How the hell should I know?"

Ned tried to cover his eyes with his arm, but it hurt too much. He turned his head to the wall. Raymond's voice became soft and earnest.

"Ned. Please. Brick is dead. You're the last chance I've got. Help me put it together, before I go crazy."

A long silence occurred while Ned considered how to answer. Raymond waited until Shoemaker turned to look him in the eye.

"Millie always protected you," he said.

Raymond's caught his breath.

"What are you saying?"

"Well, hell. Think about it. Who knew the players better than Millie?" asked Ned. "You were all her students. She knew every kid in town."

"Keep going. This ain't obvious yet."

Shoemaker took a deep breath before continuing.

"Millie knew Brick would never back off. And she knew you'd hunt him down and kill him. She also knew you'd get sent to jail for it. If I didn't do it, Bud would."

Shoemaker hesitated to let that sink in. Raymond glanced away for a moment.

"Go on," he said.

"I figure she saw the only way to end it. But things turned to shit before she could get out. I'm thinking flashover," he said.

Raymond's eyes watered and his nose began to run. He sniffed and wiped his nose. He dried his eyes with his sleeve.

"Explain, please," he said.

"Flashover. Super-heated smoke piling up against the ceiling. Can't burn because it's starved for oxygen, until … I don't know, maybe … a window breaks or something. If she was on the stairs … It's hard to say."

Raymond finally saw it. He sank into the chair and cradled his head in his fingertips. He could picture Millie coming down to the landing, gun in both hands, checking out the noise and smell of gasoline, holding Brick at gunpoint—a standoff inside a burning house. Brick must have known he was dead if he didn't move, so he bet she was bluffing.

Two quick rounds—he's down, lost in the smoke. Heat forcing her down step by step, choking, blinded by the smoke. She knows Brick is between her and the door. He catches fire and then bolts for the door. She jumps back. Fresh air rushes in … in all likelihood, by the time Ned got to Brick, Millie was gone.

Raymond spent the night talking quietly with Ned, giving the man a chance to come to grips with it all. He wanted to give him some of the comfort he himself had received from Elaine and Julius Gilmore. Raymond knew from experience that sleep will not visit the bed of those who torture themselves with guilt. The ache in his heart told him he'd never see Ned again. The pain that joined them also divided them.

CHAPTER THIRTEEN

Return Receipt Requested

Friday, September 24, 1976

Night had fallen when Sheriff Bud Oswald walked out to his truck. Raymond Thornton sat on the running board, drinking from a bottle of J&B Scotch. Neither one of them was shaven, but for different reasons.

Raymond attempted to wave but fumbled the bottle. It glanced off his boot and clattered in the gutter. When he dove after it, he toppled onto the sidewalk.

Bud reached down with his right hand and grabbed Raymond's collar. He hauled him to a standing position, taking the bottle away with his left. Then he spun him around and backed him into a sitting position on the steps.

"Mr. Thornton," he said between gritted teeth, "give me one good reason not to arrest you for public drunkenness."

Raymond waved loosely to the dark and empty streets.

"What public? We're out here all alone."

Then, hooking his heel on a step, he dropped his chin into his palm and tried to prop his elbow on his knee. He missed the first time.

"Sheriff, I kinda need to talk to you in private."

"Raymond, if you ever get plastered sitting on my truck again, I will personally haul you out to the quarry and throw you in. Do you understand me?"

Raymond waved both hands across his chest and shook his head.

"Thank you, but that won't be nesharary."

"Just what the hell is going on?" Bud asked.

Raymond stared at the sidewalk and shook his head from side to side as he spoke.

"I got a new fight coming. Donovan won't go away."

"What do you mean?" Bud said. "Brick is dead. That part is over."

"No. No, ish not."

Raymond rested his elbows on his knees, letting his arms dangle. Then he looked up at Bud, his eyes watering.

"I can't get away. Tater's stuff is all over the shop. Elaine and Julius don't need a bunch of old brushes. I was tryin' to figure out what to do with all of it when the mailman showed up. Special delivery, return resheet requested."

He pulled a yellow envelope out of his jacket pocket. His hand trembled when he held it out. Bud took the envelope.

Raymond sighed, reached for the scotch, and missed. Bud held it away from him.

"I'm all-in, partner," Raymond said.

Bud studied the envelope. It was from Garrett Stilton. He stooped down to plant the bottle on the sidewalk between his feet. Using both hands, he slipped the letter out of the envelope. He unfolded it and read it carefully. Then he took in a deep breath and let it out with a sigh.

Glancing around to be sure no one was watching, the sheriff picked up the scotch and took a quick belt before handing the bottle back to Raymond. It burnt all the way down, like swallowing a liquid barn fire. He reached into his pocket to pull out his keys.

"Get in the truck. Let's go get your things. You're going out to the cabin for a while," he said.

Raymond rose and stumbled. Bud steered him until he got him seated and closed the door.

"Don't you throw up in my truck," Bud muttered.

Then he went around to the driver's side. It would be nearly two months before Raymond Thornton haunted the streets of Raleigh again.

CHAPTER FOURTEEN

At the Cabin

Friday, November 19, 1976

For weeks, Raymond roamed the hills around Lake Osage like Legion, a man possessed. But he had neither swine nor savior to set him free. He was on his own. Some nights he ranged the hills like he was on patrol back in Vietnam. Other times he sat beneath a tree and drank until his brain shut down.

In the first few days, Bud left him stranded without transportation and without booze. Those days were the hardest because his rage consumed him from the inside out. On the nineteenth, Wally and Betty came out together. She drove their family car, and Wally drove Raymond's truck. The bed was loaded with groceries. It also included a case of scotch. It was Betty's idea to keep Raymond off the roads.

When he saw them pulling up beside the cabin, he emerged from the tree line where he had been hiding. He stood in the shade, one hand resting on a limb at shoulder height. His Levis were filthy, his flannel shirt unbuttoned, his white undershirt hanging over the .45 in his belt. When he satisfied himself they were alone, he shifted the gun to the small of his back and self-consciously buttoned his shirt. He led Wally and Betty Ann up the steps and across the deck into the living room, where they all sat down.

After a brief silence, Betty spoke.

"Raymond, you look like hell. How are you doing?"

"Okay, I guess."

He looked down, knowing it wasn't the truth.

58

"We can take guard duty while you shower and get cleaned up, if you like," she said softly.

Raymond thought it over.

"That'd be good."

He stood to head toward the bathroom.

"Do you have any clean clothes out here?" Wally asked.

"Maybe. I really haven't thought much about it," Raymond mumbled.

"Why don't you go hit the showers while I round up something for you to wear?" Wally said.

Without a word, Raymond started unbuttoning his shirt on his way to the bathroom. Wally went in to see what he could find in the closet. Betty Ann stepped outside onto the deck.

Raymond had showered and put on a different pair of jeans and a white T-shirt when she came back in. He padded barefoot around the kitchen, making coffee. Wally was still rustling around in the bedroom. Raymond glanced in to see him stuffing dirty clothes into a pillowcase. He went back to the kitchen. Betty Ann trailed behind him and leaned against the counter, her arms folded and her head cocked.

"Ray," she said, "do you know what day it is?"

He stopped scooping coffee and thought for a minute. Then he looked off into the corner toward a cluttered desk.

"No, I really don't."

"It's Friday, November 19. Next Thursday is Thanksgiving. You want to come spend the day with us?" she asked.

It could be fun. At least it would get him back in the world for a while.

"Yeah, that would be great."

"Do you have a calendar?" Betty Ann asked.

Raymond looked around. Seeing none, his eyes settled on a grocery bag from the Piggly-Wiggly. He tore it open and drew a grid, five rows by seven, and labeled it November.

"What did you say today was?" he asked.

"Friday, November 19."

Raymond picked the third Friday and wrote "19" in it. Then he numbered backward and forward until he was done. He circled the date, and then circled Thanksgiving.

"Why don't you come in on Wednesday to spend the night with us?" she asked.

"Okay. I'll be there," Raymond said.

Wally, listening from the bedroom door, held an armload of laundry. He put the laundry by the front door and walked over to lean against the kitchen door frame.

"Since you are going to be our guest of honor, what would you like to eat?" he asked.

Raymond ran his hand along his bearded cheek and then scratched his neck as he thought it over.

"Honestly? Right now? Nothing would taste better than ham, beans, and cornbread."

"That's exactly what I was going to fix," Betty said.

"It is not," Raymond said.

"Is too."

"Is not."

"You'll just have to come and see, won't you?" Betty Ann said.

She was smiling.

Raymond turned to her and put his hands on her shoulders. He looked her in the eye for the first time that night.

"Don't think for a moment I don't know what you're doing," he said. "You want me to come on Wednesday night so someone can come get me on Thursday if I don't show up. Betty, you are a sweetheart."

"Why, Mr. Thornton, I have no idea what you are talking about," Betty Ann said.

Raymond turned to look at Wally.

"Does she lie to you like this, too?" he asked.

"All the time," Wally answered. "Pretty girls can get away with it."

Raymond nodded his head. Then he gave Betty Ann a small hug and reached out for Wally's hand. As they shook, Wally gave Raymond a pat on the shoulder. Raymond recognized it as a small gesture that conveyed a big message.

"Thanks. Both of you," he said.

As they made their way to the door, Raymond had to dry his eyes with the heels of his hands. He sniffed and wiped his cheeks.

"Tell Willie and Meredith I will be there Wednesday night."

"We will do that," Wally said.

They went through another round of farewells on the deck before Wally and Betty Ann went down the steps, hand in hand. Raymond waved as they got in the car. After turning the car around, Wally gave a little toot of the horn.

Raymond rested on his elbows on the deck railing until he could no longer hear the car. An owl hooted in the distance. Apparently, everything was safe. He went out to the truck and started hauling the groceries inside. That ended when he found the scotch.

CHAPTER FIFTEEN

Thanksgiving Day

Thursday, November 25, 1976

Lucy claimed to be unconcerned about the lacerations on the back of her head and shoulders, but the sheriff wasn't buying it. Instead, he asked her to Thanksgiving dinner. She accepted. He picked her up at her home and they made small talk until they reached the Graysons' home. After he pulled into the driveway, he gave her a briefing.

"Wally and Betty Ann are good people. Their kids, Meredith and Willie, are just like their folks: good kids. It's Raymond we need to keep an eye on. Vietnam was not kind to him, and he has not taken Millie's loss lightly. We are trying to keep him from doing something stupid until he pulls himself together. I'd appreciate any observations or suggestions you might have."

"I think you're skirting another issue today," she said.

Bud looked at her and blinked, genuinely puzzled.

With a twinkle in her eye, Lucy opened the door and stepped down onto the driveway. She looked across the seat at him as she swung her bag onto her shoulder.

"Do you think these folks are ready for me?"

Bud laughed as he climbed out of the truck. He closed his door and came around to hers. He nudged it closed and took her hand in his.

"Not in the slightest," he said.

When they turned to walk toward the house, they caught a glimpse of Meredith standing at the living room window. Her mouth was open. When Bud waved, she disappeared.

"You have just been announced," he said.

Lucy had been studying the sheriff for a while. She took note of the way Bud talked to the kids. He addressed them as grown-ups. He didn't offer advice. He offered wisdom.

"Don't disregard the truth just because you don't like the source," he told them. Later she heard him say, "Always work as a team. The fellow on the other side of the clearing will see things you missed."

Lucy wondered which clearing he had in mind. She made a note to ask him on the way home. If cornbread and beans surprised her as Thanksgiving fare, she didn't let on. She liked the way she was made to feel at home, and was genuinely entertained by Raymond's many tales.

Once the kids went to bed, the adults gathered in the living room for a serious discussion. Lucy intended at first to be just a spectator. That changed in time.

"What do we know about Garrett Stilton," Bud asked, "aside from the fact that he is a complete ass?"

"He doesn't pay his bills," Wally said, cradling a cup of coffee in both hands.

"What do you mean?"

"He still owes me money for groceries. He gave me a sob story, and I fell for it. I have sent him bills, but he doesn't answer."

Betty looked at him in surprise.

"You never told me that," Betty said. Wally shrugged.

Lucy liked what she saw in these people.

"What do we know about Brick's mom?" Bud asked.

No else one seemed to have any information, so Lucy shared what she knew.

"She's in the state hospital," she said. "She pickled her brain drinking. They found her living under a bridge, loony as could be. The courts eventually declared her incompetent, and she became a ward of the state."

"How do you know all that?" Betty asked.

"I worked for a while in the women's shelter. She came through the system. She was one of the saddest cases we ever saw."

"So what are the chances Brick's death has caused her irreparable harm?" asked Bud.

"He used to beat her," Lucy said. "That's why she was living under the bridge while he was in his mama's house alone. I don't see her as the grief-stricken mother, but that doesn't keep Stilton from dressing her up for court and having her dab at her eyes with a monogrammed hanky."

Betty's eyes got wide as she listened. Wally kept an eye on Raymond, who seemed to sink into the couch. He was scowling.

"This brings us back to the question of Stilton. He's really gambling on this one," Bud said.

"So how do we get him to drop the suit?" Raymond asked. "Or do I just go kill him in the middle of the night?"

"Not the best plan so far," Bud said.

Lucy spoke up again, this time with little hesitation.

"He is a sick man. His wife came through the system, too. I know why she left."

Everyone looked at her.

"Go on," said Bud.

"His idea of foreplay included clamps, needles, and lit cigarettes. I took pictures in case Nettie wanted to press charges."

"What happened?" Raymond asked.

"He caved in when a case worker showed up on his doorstep with the photos."

"What did he say to him?" Wally asked.

"She. It was a woman. A big woman. Two hundred pounds of 'Don't give me none of your bullshit.' She described to him in very clear terms what would happen to him if Nettie pressed charges. She told him how, inside the big-house, sex offenders get to wear fishnet stockings on Saturday night. She got in his face and he peed in his pants."

"Are you telling me that this guy is actually afraid of women?" asked Raymond.

"No. He's afraid of women with power. Guys like him are cowards. Female authority figures scare them. It's like their Mama is going after them with a frying pan. That's why they choose submissive girls. They can push them around and feel powerful," Lucy explained.

There was a long silence while everyone considered what Lucy just told them.

"Sounds like I should go kill him in the middle of the night," Raymond said.

No one argued with him this time. Finally Wally spoke up.

"Well, look, does Stilton have a case or not?" he asked.

"Put it in context," answered Bud. "Strip away all the extraneous stuff. Millie shoots Brick, that could be murder one. The fact that he also died from burns, not just bullets, helps a lot. Put them in a burning building, and it changes things. Is the fire a direct threat to her life? Does he give her some other reason to defend herself? If we include the bombing downtown and Tater's shooting, things go to an extreme. Clearly with all that, he was a dangerous man."

"So why all the fuss?" Wally asked.

"The fight will be to see what gets into court and what doesn't," Bud explained. "Stilton will want to exclude everything but the shooting. The lawyer for the estate will need to bring in all the other stuff to show that Brick was so dangerous that just finding him in your house is reason enough to shoot him."

"Aw, hell. I think I'm going to throw up," Raymond said.

"Wait a minute here," said Betty Ann. "The case worker got through to him with a little 'come to Jesus' meeting. If it worked once, maybe it can work again. Maybe he just needs a strong woman to explain it to him."

Everyone looked at Lucy.

"Can I wear a gun?" she asked.

"You bet," Bud answered. "And a badge. For this, I will deputize you. We can even hang some cuffs on your belt if it will help."

"I'll do it. But I'm going to need some things for show-and-tell."

"Tell me what you need."

CHAPTER SIXTEEN

A Visitation

Friday, November 26, 1976

Lucy looked up the dark stairway toward Stilton's office. She was jittery. Then she remembered Nettie and Millie. She let her anger build with each step she climbed.

Lucy yanked open the door and stepped up to Garrett Stilton's desk. She reached down with one finger and cut off his telephone call in the middle of a conversation.

Her eyes bored into him.

"I'm sorry," she said. "This will only take a moment of your time."

Stilton's mouth dropped open and he began to rise in protest. She rested one hand on her gun and waved the clipboard in her other hand at the chair.

"Sit your sorry ass down, shut your mouth, and listen to what I am about to tell you. You want the whole world to know you only have one testicle?"

His face flushed and blood vessels bulged in his neck.

"I'll have you know I have both my testicles!"

Lucy placed both hands on her hips and faced him squarely.

"Don't worry. You won't when I'm done with you. Now sit down, shut up, and listen!"

The lawyer sank back into his chair in total confusion, dropping the telephone handset back in the cradle. Lucy peeled back some papers to examine something on her clipboard.

"Did you file a wrongful death lawsuit against the estate of Margaret Millicent McKenna Thornton?"

Stilton nodded his head and started to smirk.

"Maybe this will amuse you," she said, tossing an eight-by-ten color photo of what was left of a black man's face on an autopsy table. "This is what Brick Donovan did to Tater Gilmore."

Stilton looked down at the picture and then turned pale. His eyes bulged and his mouth gaped open as he tried to make sense of what he saw.

"This is what Brick Donovan did to the sheriff," she said as she placed an emergency room photo of Bud's lacerated face in front of him. "You know, he's a nice guy and all, but he took it kinda personal."

The lawyer winced.

"This is what Brick did to the sheriff's truck," she said, dealing out another photo.

Stilton scowled.

"And this is what he did to me," she said, plunking down a photo of her bare back, neck, and shaved head, showing lacerations spreading like lace across her body. She took off her sunglasses and bent over to get in Stilton's face.

"So we have taken a special interest in this case, if you know what I mean."

He could smell coffee and anger on her breath. Garrett swallowed.

"Now, to win in court, your client will need to gain the sympathy of the judge and jury. There's one problem, though. Brick's autopsy indicates the gunshot wounds may have been survivable. His cause of death included lung damage and burns, a direct result of his own actions. At least, that is the way our expert is going to pitch it. Are you following me, here?"

"Now, see here, young lady …"

Lucy placed her left hand in the middle of his desk and leaned over. She slapped him hard. He started to speak. She nailed him again, this time even harder.

"Do *not* interrupt me when I am explaining the real shit to you," she said.

Then she tossed another photo on his desk.

"And this is what was left of Margaret Millicent McKenna Thornton after your client set her house on fire," she said. "That is what we call in the business a 'crispy critter.'"

Lucy watched him turn green. He was going to vomit. She grabbed his trash can and thumped it down by his chair just in time. She waited for him to finish. It took awhile. He lifted his head, face dripping with sweat, wiping spittle from his mouth with the back of his hand. Then she continued.

"Naturally, it will be important to establish a timeline leading up to the shooting, so the sheriff and I will be key witnesses. That's the kind of civic-minded folks we are. I believe in the whole truth, don't you? I have dedicated my life to it."

She studied him for a moment. Then she put her sunglasses back on.

"So whatcha think? Is it realistic to believe a lame-ass lawyer like you can win the sympathy of the court in a case like this? Or would you be better off spending your time elsewhere?"

Stilton slumped down in his chair, his face turned away from the pictures strewn across his desk. He made a sweeping motion with one hand, burped, and fought back the nausea.

"Please," he said weakly, his voice raspy, "take them away."

Lucy gathered them up, tapped them into a neat stack on his desk, and put them back on the clipboard. She walked to the door. Then she stopped and wheeled to face him again. She pointed the clipboard at him.

"Oh, yeah. There is something else I should tell you."

"Yeah?"

"Those two slaps back there?"

"Yeah?" he said, touching his cheek.

"Those were for Nettie. I worked in the women's shelter when she left you. I took pictures of what you did to her. Really ugly pictures.

It would probably be best for all concerned if that information didn't leak out, don'tcha think?"

She opened the door and stepped into the hall. Then she leaned back in.

"You may want to call that person back and apologize for the interruption. Sorry."

She slammed the door firmly and waited outside, listening. After a long period of silence, she descended the steps. By now she was on the shaky side of an adrenaline rush. Still, by the time she stepped back out into the daylight, she was practically giddy with exhilaration, amazed at her own audacity. It had felt so damned good!

Bud stood at the curb.

"How did it go?" he asked, opening the passenger door of his truck.

"Tell you in a minute," she said, unwilling to discuss it on the street. She climbed into the truck and then swung her knees in so he could close the door.

Bud checked traffic, went around to the driver's door, and then got in. He started the engine and then drove away. He waited for her to speak.

"Well?" he finally said.

She was still playing it back in her mind.

"I slapped him."

"What?"

"Twice. For Nettie."

"Oh, sweet Jesus!"

"You know what else?"

"I'm afraid to ask."

"Garrett Stilton only has one testicle."

"What?"

She held up her fist.

"I got the other one right here."

CHAPTER SEVENTEEN

Suspicious Behavior

Wednesday, December 1, 1976

Melanie watched the battle-scarred Lincoln pull into the lot and turn around. The driver backed up against the fence and parked, hood ornament aimed at the gate. An overweight man with his hair combed back and a rumpled suit opened the door and struggled to get both feet on the ground. With considerable effort, he pushed himself to a standing position and headed toward the office, slamming the car door behind him.

He walked funny. Melanie started analyzing it. By the time he reached the door, she had a theory. He walked with his feet splayed out. One foot seemed floppy, and the leg on that side moved awkwardly. If she had to guess, she'd say hamstring.

At first Melanie felt a twinge of sympathy. Carrying extra weight was hard enough. Then she realized he had packed on the weight in spite of his bum leg. Bad idea. She swiveled her chair to face the door. She watched through the window as he hobbled up the steps and shouldered his way into the office. She popped her gum at him when he entered.

"How's your golf game?" she asked.

He looked around with a sniff of disgust.

"I don't play games," he snarled. "Where's Junior?"

"Too bad. All we do here is play games. It's a laugh a minute," Melanie said.

She aimed her thumb over her shoulder and blew bubbles at the guy as he passed. She was pretty sure nobody but a lawyer would come out here. This had to be the guy folks called Tiltin' Stilton.

She declared herself on-duty. She pulled out a yellow legal pad and began to scribble. Junior couldn't read short-hand, so she frequently wrote everything down word-for-word.

Old man Petiole had always been an honest drunkard, but Junior put him to shame. He kept poor company and fought often. Dishonorably discharged from the Marines even before finishing boot camp, his life was a string of brawls and loose women. Legal problems did not surprise Melanie. What struck her was the paranoia.

Junior had always been loud. Right now, he sat in his office whispering. More importantly, the lawyer was giving orders. She pulled out a parts catalog, opened the switch on the intercom, and adjusted the volume to eavesdrop. She pretended to look up part numbers while writing down what she heard. She had no trouble understanding most of it, because she had a lot of practice.

"Don't jerk me around, Junior. I know too much," she heard the lawyer say. Melanie cocked an eyebrow and wrote it down. She heard the squeak of Junior's chair swiveling back and forth.

"I got you by the balls and you know it," the lawyer continued. "So don't give me any static. Just be at the airport before daybreak on Friday and get the package out of the trash bin. Then do like I say. If you don't want any drivers in on it then drive the rig yourself. I don't give a shit. I just want the stuff delivered first thing in the morning."

Melanie wrote fast. Junior's voice seemed almost meek. That really got Melanie's attention. She strained to make out his answer.

"One time, right? I'll do it just this once because I owe you. But that's it, Goddammit," Junior said softly.

"You're not hearing me, JP. You're damn right you owe me. Truth is, I own you. And that's why you're gonna do what I say, when I say, from now on until forever. Am I making myself clear?"

Melanie heard Junior's chair swiveling and the thump of his elbows on the desk.

"Jeez, yeah, okay, okay. Just get out of here before Porky starts connecting the dots. Don't be coming in here like this."

She heard the broken-down couch in Junior's office groan under a shifting load and the shuffling of feet. When the lawyer spoke again, his voice boomed out over the speaker. He must be hovering right over the intercom. Melanie quickly turned down the volume.

"Right. Go ahead," the lawyer said. "Do ten-to-twenty. No problem. I'll leave now and let the DA dredge up whatever he finds. It's your life. You've got until Friday."

Melanie jumped when Junior's office door opened. The fat man in the bad suit hobbled past her desk, aimed at the exit. He glanced over at her. She kept thumbing through the parts catalog. He didn't see her switch off the intercom with her left hand because the tattered binder blocked his view. When she looked up, he glared at her. She flashed him a big smile, blew a bubble, and then popped it.

"Keep your putter clean," she said.

He slammed the door behind him without a word. Through Junior's open office door, she could see him sitting behind his desk with his head in his hands. Melanie gave him two minutes. He would leave for the rest of the day.

Junior stood and pulled his tattered parka off the coat rack behind him. He stepped out into the outer office and shoved one arm into a sleeve.

"You're in charge," Junior said. "I've got some business to do. Anything comes up, take care of it."

As Junior fished for the other sleeve, Melanie spotted the empty shoulder holster.

"Did you forget something?" she said, pointing with her pencil.

Junior slapped at his side and went back into the office. She watched him pull a gun out of his drawer, check the cylinder, snap it shut, and slip it into the holster. Then he went straight for the door.

"Don't forget to bring me a present," she said

"Go to hell."

"Love you, too."

Most of the time, Junior swore and waved his arms. Melanie noticed this time he had both hands buried in his pockets and was staring at the ground as he walked out to the car. Whatever was going on, this was big. She checked the parking lot to make sure no one else was around before she picked up the phone. Melanie no longer needed to look up Bud's number.

CHAPTER EIGHTEEN

The Tip

Wednesday, December 1, 1976

Sheriff Oswald stood on the sidewalk, listening to a local farmer's view of the recent presidential election.

"Hell of a choice is all I'm saying," the farmer said. "What's it gonna be, the guy who pardoned Nixon, or a peanut farmer from Georgia? What kind of message does that send to the world, you know what I mean?"

Bud was nodding his head when he heard Lucy's voice paging him on the radio.

"Excuse me," Bud said. "I'd better see what this is about."

He reached in through the open driver's window of his truck to retrieve the mike. He pulled it to him, stretching the cord out the window, and thumbed the key.

"Roger, dispatch. Sheriff here. Go ahead."

"A female caller says she has some urgent information for you."

"Stand by. Give me a second before you patch her through," he said. "I'm in front of Dutch's Diner, so I need to get inside the truck first."

"Roger. Say when," said Lucy.

Bud climbed in behind the wheel and pulled the door closed.

"Here we go," he said. "Let me roll up the window … okay, patch her through."

"Roger. Go ahead, ma'am. I have the sheriff on the line."

"Bud, is that you?"

"Yes. Go ahead."

"You know who this is?"

"I recognize your voice."

"Okay. Here's what I got. A fat gimpy guy paid Junior a visit this morning. Told him to pick up a package in the airport trash bin Friday morning, or else."

Bud shoved his hat back on his head.

"Describe the guy."

"About six feet, two hundred seventy, eighty pounds or so. Long hair combed back, bad suit. Drives an old Lincoln beater, and walks like an elephant with three legs."

"Wait. What's the problem when he walks?"

"One floppy foot. Kinda has to throw it out in front of him just to take the next step," Melanie said. "Is that Tiltin' Stilton?"

"Sounds like it," Bud said. "So what makes this urgent?"

"What the hell's wrong with you? Don't you get it? Somebody's making a drop-off, and Junior has to deliver. What do you want? A bag of doughnuts to go with it?"

Bud scouted the streets out of force of habit. He wasn't sure he was ready to buy in.

"Melanie, you are a piece of work. Anybody ever tell you that?"

"Not since prom night."

"So, how solid is this?" Bud asked. "You're asking me to send a deputy out all night to sit on a dumpster. What does he tell his wife, I got garbage detail at the airport tonight?"

Bud heard Melanie shifting her weight around in the chair and then the familiar slurping of coffee. Her cup thumped the desk when she put it down.

"Tell her that Stilton was mean, angry, and threatening."

"Now there's a piece of news."

"Tell her that Junior was rattled enough to forget his gun."

Bud sat up and thought that over. He did a quick 360 survey of his surroundings. Junior may be just plain stupid and mean, but he wasn't someone you'd expect to get rattled.

"When was the last time you saw him scared?"

"Never."

"Okay, Melanie. I got it. Not a word, okay? Not to your cousin, not to your grandpa, not to anybody. You need to be careful."

"Don't worry about me. I can take care of myself. I don't go nowhere without an equalizer," she said.

Bud thought about that. He didn't like it.

"If that means what I think it means, I don't want to know about it."

"Okay. I lied. I am helpless."

"Good … Melanie?"

"Yeah?"

"You have any idea what's in the package?"

"Not the slightest."

"Okay. Thanks."

The line went dead.

"Lucy, did you get that?" Bud asked.

"All of it."

"Okay. We'll talk later. Over."

"Roger. Out."

Bud drove back to the office. He climbed the stairs and entered the dispatch room. Elaine and Lucy looked up to see what was going on. Silently, he pointed to the county topographical map on the wall. Then he walked over to stand in front of it. He rubbed his chin as he thought. He had never paid much attention to the Raleigh Municipal Airport. Now he studied it carefully.

Two runways crisscrossed, one paved and one grass. The paved runway ran southwest to northeast. The grass runway intersected the main runway midfield. He noticed all of the buildings and hangars were on the northeast corner of the airport property. That's where the trash containers would be. Satisfied, he turned to leave, waving to the dispatchers on his way out. He left without saying a word. Lucy knew exactly what he was doing.

Bud drove out to the airport to look around. He had been to the flight operations building a few times, but it was usually to provide security for a visiting politician. He found it unnerving to realize how unfamiliar he was with this section of his county. That would have to change.

A slow drive around the airport revealed a trash bin behind the maintenance hangar, another by the flight operations building, and two fifty-five-gallon drums, one on the ramp beside the gas pumps, and another behind the Prop'n'Wing flying club hangar. The only way to find out which trash bin was the target would be to sit on the airport overnight. Bud began developing a plan. Because Melanie's tip was so thin, he decided to do it himself.

As night fell, Bud drove his pickup along the gravel lane opposite the airport entrance. He drove in underneath some trees out of sight of the road. Then he parked the truck, removed the light bulb from the dome light, and rolled both windows down a few inches to listen. He pulled an old army blanket over himself for warmth and concealment. He had plenty of gas in the tank, so he could use the heater if needed. He placed a set of field glasses on the seat beside him. It would be a long night.

Not quite an hour into his vigil, a plane entered the traffic pattern and made five or six touch-and-go landings before taxiing to the ramp. It shut down in front of the club hangars. A door opened on the right side, and he watched a local dentist and flight instructor climb out over the wing. They departed the airport in separate cars shortly after nine. Bud relaxed into the sound of the night, allowing himself to catnap while listening for any changes.

The drone of an approaching aircraft almost slipped up on him. The Doppler shift woke him as the plane passed overhead. He checked the time: 1:43 AM. He was startled when the runway lights came on, and momentarily lost track of the airplane. He had to climb out of the truck to find it again. It crossed midfield and turned left to parallel the paved runway. The engine hushed, and a beam of light suddenly stabbed out into the darkness. This was it. He ran for the road.

When the aircraft entered a descending left turn, Bud rose and dashed across the highway to the airport parking lot. He cut toward the row of shade hangars. Advancing toward the runway, he found an unobstructed view of the flight line. He dove beneath the belly of a Piper twin that, judging from the bird droppings, hadn't flown in decades. He lifted the field glasses and followed the airplane as it lined up with the runway.

The high-winged plane settled silently and flared over the pavement. Soon he heard the distant chirp of rubber on asphalt. The plane slowed, turned around on the runway, and then added power to taxi back toward the ramp. It was a Cessna. When it turned off the runway, the pilot shut down all the lights, killed the engine and let the aircraft coast in darkness toward the pumps. Just short of the pumps the plane turned to the right and stopped. Bud could hear the tires crunching across the snow. His teeth chattered. He shifted around to keep the trash barrel in view and waited.

In the faint glow of the runway lights, he saw the pilot's door open. A figure got out and headed to the barrel. Bud heard a thump and watched the pilot hurry back to the plane, climb in, start the engine, and then head back toward the runway.

When the tail was pointing directly at him, he rose to sprint across uneven ground toward the departure end of the runway. He needed to make out the numbers painted on the fuselage.

The plane reached the turn-around and did a tight 180 before hitting the lights. Bud dropped into the grass and remained motionless. The engine roared and the Cessna accelerated in a cloud of snow down the runway. It rose into the sky.

Bud stood up, brushed himself off, and then walked back across the road, repeating the tail number out loud again and again until he had it memorized. The next part would be easier. He returned to the truck to sit behind the wheel, engine idling and heater blasting.

He got out a pen and flashlight to write everything down. With the windows cracked slightly, he could not miss the sound of an approaching garbage truck. The sun did not appear until a little after seven thirty.

Soon after daybreak, he heard the big rig coming. The Packmaster drove by and turned into the airport parking lot. It headed straight for the trash bin behind the maintenance hangar. Bud knew it was Junior when he heard him swearing and stomping around in the trash bin. After a ten-minute search, he climbed back out. Then he hauled himself back up into the cab. He was not happy.

The truck crossed to the dumpster behind flight ops, where Junior repeated his performance. He was harder to hear from this distance, but Bud could tell it was not going well. He felt sorry for the guy, but he couldn't very well stroll over and say, "Try the barrel on the flight line." Instead, he had to wait for Junior to figure it out on his own.

Eventually, a dirty, grumpy Junior Petiole climbed out of the second dumpster. The moment his feet hit the ground, he began swearing and waving his arms. In the process, he turned to face the ramp and spotted the trash barrel beside the pumps. He clambered back up into the garbage truck and drove out onto the ramp in front of the pumps. He braked to a stop and jumped down from the cab, skittering across the snow to the barrel. He fished out a leather satchel and climbed back into the cab. Then he roared off the airport, snow and trash swirling in the air behind him. Bud got a glimpse of him wiping sweat from his brow with his left arm as he drove past.

There was no way to follow a slow-moving garbage truck without being conspicuous. The sheriff had endured enough for one night. It was time to go home, take a long shower, and go into the office. He needed a hot cup of coffee and a thoughtful conversation with Lucy.

CHAPTER NINETEEN

Blue-Belle Dry Cleaning

Friday, December 3, 1976

A few minutes after eight, Clyde Dewey sloshed down the alley in his overshoes. He fished around in his pocket for the key to unlock the back door. Then he let himself in.

At fifty-four, he walked like a man in his seventies. Years of fumes had taken their toll. He was rail thin with a dowager's hump. He face was gaunt, with brown leathery skin that made him look like a walking mummy. Food hadn't had flavor in years—not since his wife died.

He pulled open the door and stepped inside. He tossed his sandwich in the small fridge in the break room before going back outside. Pulling the lid off the garbage can, he found it empty except for a satchel lying in the bottom. He began to lean in to retrieve it, but got a whiff of garbage and decided against it. He went back inside for a coat hanger. He twisted it into a hook to snag the handle. He expected the satchel to be heavy. It wasn't. Folding the hanger into a wad, he dropped it into the can, replaced the lid, and then slipped back inside before anyone noticed what he was doing.

Clyde toed off his galoshes and hung up his overcoat before walking into the tiny office. He dropped the leather bag on his desk and fished through the drawer for the key. It wasn't much of a latch, it wasn't much of a key, and it didn't matter anyway. Someone had cut the strap. Inside were three stuffed brown envelopes, each sealed at the flap with packing tape. One of them had been sliced open at the bottom. When pictures fell out, he looked.

In the first, a naked man and woman stood in water up to their knees, startled faces frozen by the pop of a flashbulb, caught in mid-turn toward the camera. The man looked familiar.

Clyde studied the face more closely. He checked the rest of the photographs, and realized they were all of the same man, but not necessarily the same occasion or the same woman. The man in the pictures looked like Senator Randall William Stennis, chairman of the Armed Services Committee. Hastily, he shoved the photos back in the envelope and taped it shut.

Waves of nausea rolled over him. He began to hyperventilate. Holding his breath, he forced himself to calm down and think this through. Stilton had told him to put this stuff in his safe deposit box. Clyde had the only key. Who else would know? It was clear the lawyer wasn't going to touch it because he didn't want dirt on his hands.

Clyde mulled this over. Maybe he should just do what Stilton said and keep his mouth shut. He had enough trouble as it was. He swiveled back and forth in his chair and looked around. He didn't remember the place being this grimy. During the past twelve years, he hadn't bothered to keep up the back end. Keeping the front end spotless mattered to the public. *Thank goodness, they have no idea what goes on back here.*

He looked at the ruined satchel. It wouldn't fit in the safe deposit box anyway. He dropped it into the wastebasket beside his desk and stared at the envelopes. He stood and went up front to get a shirt box. On the lid, a bunny in a uniform saluted and said, "Thanks for your business!" He took it back to his desk and put the envelopes inside.

With a sigh, he forced himself to think about opening the store today. He sorted and checked the tags on the clothing that came in yesterday afternoon and started a load of dry cleaning. Then he turned on the pressing irons and went out front to straighten up. Della would be in soon, and he could go to the bank.

She didn't show up by opening time. She hadn't been well lately. Clyde picked up the little sign with the clock face and set the moveable hands to nine fifteen. He hung it in the front door, and locked up with his key. With less than a block to go, he had ample time.

He tried to act nonchalant when the teller at the bank asked him to sign in. He held the box crammed with envelopes away from her like a schoolboy hiding a note. She led him into the vault, her key in one hand.

"Clyde, are you feeling okay?" she asked.

That was one of the problems of living in a small town. Everybody knew your name. She was young and pretty. He tried to remember her father. He wondered if she was married now. He was good with faces, but lousy with names.

"Yeah, sure, I'm fine. Why do you ask?"

"I don't know. You just seem a little … peaked."

He thought about that while he fished out his key and handed it to her. He felt nauseous. Beads of sweat began to pop out. She would be mortified to know what he was carrying right now. His mouth was dry. He licked his lips.

"Oh, you think so? I guess I am worried about Della. She hasn't come in yet, and I was thinking I need to give her a call."

"That explains it. Let me get your box so you can get back to the store."

After she placed the metal box on the table in the privacy room and left, Clyde quickly transferred the envelopes. Then he stepped out to catch her eye. He watched nervously when she put the box back in place. He held his hand out for his key even before she locked the door. He slipped the key into his pocket and wheeled to leave.

"Tell Della I said hello," she said.

He answered over his shoulder.

"Sure thing," Clyde said.

He shoved his way through the door before she could ask him to sign out. He scurried back to the store to get the cleaning sorted.

The call Clyde had been dreading came a little after noon. He tried to act like it was just any other day, but Garrett Stilton detected something in his voice that gave him away.

"You sound funny," Stilton said. "Are you sure everything went all right?"

"Yeah, sure, everything's okay. It's all sealed just like you said. It's in the bank box now just like you wanted … all safe and sound … no problems … lots of room. No one else will ever know."

Clyde spent the rest of the conversation agreeing with everything Stilton said just to get him off the line. When he hung up the phone, he realized he had a raging headache. He walked back into the overheated work area and wandered over to the spotting bench. The lipstick on the choir robe would require something special.

He opened the cabinet where he kept his secret stash and looked inside. It held every kind of solvent known to man, including carbon tetrachloride and a jar of white gasoline. Some of the stuff was illegal now, but Clyde was a collector, especially if it worked. A fifty-five-gallon drum of perchloroethylene stood beside the cabinet. He used it in the big Martin cleaner.

He pulled out a can of benzene and carried it over to the spotting bench. Then he took a deep breath and held it in while he walked over to the washer to pull a load of perc-saturated clothing out into a cart. He rolled the fuming pile of clothes across the floor, transferred it into the drying machine, and pushed the button. Then he scurried back to the spotting bench where he could exhale and resume breathing. By now, the back door stood ajar and all the fans were running.

Dewey figured the renters were right. He watched his wife waste away slowly. Now, it was getting to Della. For that matter, he didn't feel so good himself. He would have to do something soon, but he didn't know what. One thing was certain. He was just scraping by. New machines, ventilators, and a vapor system were out of the question. Time was running out. He talked to himself while he worked.

"One day this place is going to blow sky-high. I've got to get rid of some of that shit. As sick as the girl has been, small wonder the fumes have been getting to her."

As far as he was concerned, the American dream was going to hell in a hand basket. First came Vietnam. Then the riots. Then *Silent Spring,* and the EPA. Then, to top it off, OSHA wanted to put the little guy out of business.

"People want clean clothes, it's gonna take solvents. I mean, what the hell do you want? Besides, I am losing a good employee. Folks upstairs start talking about a lawsuit, and now I have friends I don't need like Stilton."

Clyde was getting light-headed and starting to sweat. Time for a break. He made a quick trip to the bathroom and then stepped into the alley for a smoke. When he lit up, he realized he was so sick of this shit he could almost drink white gas and light up a cigar. He shivered in the cold, took a long drag on his Marlboro, and waited for his head to clear.

CHAPTER TWENTY

Where to Begin

Friday, December 3, 1976

Bud sat with his heels on his desk, staring out the window at the falling snow. He had both hands on his head. He wished he had been able to follow that damn truck, but if Junior had spotted him he would be back to square one. He ran his hands through his hair and blew out his breath in frustration. Right now, all he had was an aircraft tail number and Junior Petiole. He turned to look at Sam and Lucy.

"So what do you think?" Bud said.

Sam smirked as he leaned against a file cabinet. He was up to mischief.

"Too bad you don't have an invisible truck," he said. "It would be nice to know where he went."

Bud tore a sheet of paper off a legal tablet, squeezed it into a ball, and threw it at him. Sam ducked. The wad of paper bounced off his shoulder onto the floor.

Lucy leaned out of her chair and scooped it up. She pitched it into the wastebasket on the opposite side of the room.

She shook her finger at them and scolded in her best teacher's voice.

"Recess is over, boys. Let's get back to algebra," she said.

Lucy folded her arms and looked at Bud in mock disapproval.

"Now, Bud, you apologize. And, Sam, quit smirking. You're next."

"Samuel, I am terribly sorry," Bud said with exaggerated sincerity. "I'll get right on that invisible truck thing."

Lucy looked at Sam.

"It's your turn."

"Sorry, Bud," he said. "But it would be nice to know what it was and who got it."

"Yeah, well," Bud said, "I guess a judge wouldn't mind me pulling him over to ask, 'What you got in this bag here?' Any other ideas?"

"Could it be drugs? Garbage trucks would be a great way to make deliveries."

"I thought about that," Bud said. "But Stilton went out to the dump in daylight. With Melanie there, that's like cutting a drug deal in front of city hall."

He turned to look at Lucy. Her hair had grown out enough that she quit wearing the wig. On her, a crew-cut was a good look.

"What do you think?" he asked her.

"If it is a pipeline, they will use it again," she said. "It will become a pattern. For now, it's a one-time thing. With three to four thousand possible destinations, I'm not sure an invisible truck would help that much. I say look for something out of place, work backward, and see if it connects."

Bud drummed his fingers on his desk and looked from one to the other. Sam shrugged.

"So that's it then," said Bud. "We go about our business and wait and see. Any other ideas, Sam?"

"Did you ID the aircraft? That may tell us something. Otherwise, I think Lucy is right. We wait to see what else comes down the pipeline."

Bud rocked back in his chair.

"I called the airport manager this morning to get information from the guy's flight plan," he said. "I thought all planes had to file one. Turns out it is not that simple."

"Really?" Lucy said. "Why is that?"

"The guy I talked to said there are two sets of rules, one for instruments and another for visual flying."

"Now I'm confused," Sam said.

"If I got this right, all airlines file instrument flight plans," Bud said. "Private pilots only need to do it when the weather is bad. Otherwise, they can use visual flight rules - see and avoid. The difference is whether you navigate on your own or under air traffic control."

Lucy leaned back to take that in.

"But they are required to file some kind of flight plan, aren't they?" Lucy asked.

Bud pulled a pen out of his pocket and fiddled with it. His eyebrows rose.

"Nope. He said all a visual flight plan does is trigger a search and rescue effort if you don't show up," Bud said. "The guy said he can fly from one coast to the other without ever filing a flight plan or even talking to air traffic control."

"Jesus," said Sam. "That's kinda loose. It's like a bunch of hippies piling into a VW bus and just taking off. So what do you get with the registration number?"

"It's like a license plate. It gives you the owner," Bud said, "but that's all. It doesn't tell you who flew it, or where it came from."

"So how do you find out?"

"I have to call the FAA when we get done here. I want to confirm what the guy at the airport said. Fact of the matter is I don't know a damned thing about airplanes. I am going to have to fix that," Bud said. "So what else should we be considering here?"

Sam turned to look out the window at the snow.

"How about Melanie? Is she good for more information?" he asked

"I think so," Bud said. "She wants Junior out of her life. She'll keep helping us until we send him away for good."

"What's that all about?" Lucy asked.

"They're second cousins. Something happened when she was just a kid," Bud said. "The family kept it secret. The next time he tried to mess with her, she pulled a knife and cut him."

"What happened?" she asked.

"Nothing. His daddy told him he had it coming. The Petioles keep things in the family. And they play for keeps."

"Ouch. Tough lady," said Sam.

"On the outside, maybe. But inside … I don't know. I've known her since first grade. She used to be a sweet kid, but that's all changed. We agree on one thing, though."

"What's that?"

"Junior deserves whatever he gets. Like thirty-five to forty."

They sat quietly for a moment before Lucy pointed out the window.

"Looks like we're gonna get busy."

Sam and Bud swung around to look, and saw the snowfall turning into a blizzard. Cars were going to start sliding into ditches all over the county.

"Sam, you start calling the others in. We're going to need them. Lucy, I guess you'd better get back to dispatch and let them know. Here we go, folks. Business as usual," Bud said, reaching for the phone. "I'll call the state patrol to see what's happening to the west of us." For the moment, Junior Petiole's mysterious contraband was on the back burner.

After checking the road reports with the highway patrol, Bud had an idea.

"Say, can I ask another question?" he asked.

"Sure."

"You guys have airplanes, right?"

"Yes, we do."

"Do you have a phone number for someone at the FAA who can tell me about aircraft registration numbers?"

"You probably want to talk to Flight Standards. Which number do you want, St. Louis or Kansas City?"

Bud made one more call before heading out into the snow. He got out a pencil and legal pad to make notes and wrote down the date and time of the call.

"Flight Standards. Daryl Cooke, how may I he'p you?"

"Inspector, this is Sheriff Bud Oswald, Raleigh County. How do I check out the registration on an aircraft that flew in here last night?"

"By callin' me. Any chance you got a tail number?"

"I did. You ready to copy?"

"Yep."

"N, as in Nancy, five zero eight three two."

"November."

"What?"

"In aviator talk, we call it November. Means it's a U.S. registration. November five zero eight three two. Was there an accident?" inspector Cooke asked.

"No. It just flew in here the middle of the night and took off again. It just seemed odd," Bud said.

"Could be anything," inspector Cooke said. "Night freight guy landing at the wrong airport; student on a cross-country; somebody heading home for Christmas; or somebody running dope."

"Now you know why I called," Bud said.

"Let me check the microfiche and I'll get back to you. What's your number?"

Bud gave it to him and glanced out the window again.

"Look, we have a big snow storm rolling in," Bud said. "I may be out of the office most of the day. We have a dispatcher named Lucy. When you call back, can you give her the information?"

"Sure thing," said inspector Cooke. "Try to stay out of the ditches."

"That's the general plan. Thanks."

Sheriff Bud didn't get back into the office until well after dark. When he saw Lucy's extensive notes, he suggested they go over to Dutch's Diner to get something to eat. She clocked out. Then she picked up her notes, her purse, and her coat. Without thinking, Bud helped her into her coat. He also opened all the doors for her. Lucy took note.

Lucy pulled out her notes and briefed him.

"N50832 is registered to a corporation in Delaware. Apparently a lot of people do that to create a tax shelter."

"How does that work, exactly?" Bud asked. He added cream and sugar to his coffee.

"They form a corporation and lease the plane back to somebody. Then they write off all the expenses. Inspector Cooke has given check rides in this plane at a flight school in the Bootheel. He called to ask them about it."

"What did he learn?" Bud asked.

He stirred his cream and sugar until the coffee was a walnut brown.

"It is out on a cross-country flight. According to the schedule book, they think it is being flown by an instructor named Andy Russell."

He pushed his glasses back up on his nose.

"They think?" he asked.

"A lot of folks have keys to the building," she explained. "Also, it is a common practice to hide keys inside the airplane for after-hours flights. Sort of an honor system."

Bud propped his elbow on the table and spread his hands wide in astonishment.

"You mean to tell me they really don't know where that airplane is right now?"

"Not until it comes back," Lucy said.

Bud looked across the restaurant to think about what he had just heard.

"You know, Lucy, I don't know a damned thing about aviation. None of this makes much sense to a guy who tells people every day not to leave their keys in the car."

"I couldn't believe it either."

"So how do we play catch up? We're never going to get ahead of this thing if we don't understand airplanes."

Bud put his hand to his forehead.

"I'll tell you what," she said, "maybe I can find a local flight instructor who can fill us in. We don't need to know how to fly planes, but we sure could use some help understanding how all this works."

"That's a great idea. We'll buy the guy lunch or something, just to make it worth his time."

They thought about that. Bud sipped his coffee and noticed Lucy drank hers black. It was the same color as her hair.

"Lucy, you hair is growing back nicely. It looks good."

She got a twinkle in her eye.

"Why, thank you, Sheriff. Was that a professional or personal opinion?"

Bud felt trapped. He was on unfamiliar ground.

"Both, I guess," he said.

"Well then, how about dinner? Is this professional or personal?"

She seemed to enjoy making him squirm. Bud cleared his throat.

"Both, I guess."

"Gosh, for a man who likes to get to the facts, you sure are doing a lot of guessing."

She chuckled before taking a sip of coffee. There was mischief in her eye.

He relaxed and smiled. Then she leaned forward and spoke quietly.

"We both might enjoy ourselves more if we could learn to leave our work at the office. I'm thinking we can drop the professional part for the rest of the evening."

Bud read her eyes. What he saw was encouraging.

"Does that make this sort of a first date?" he asked.

"God, I hope so," she laughed. "I wasn't sure Thanksgiving counted."

For the first time in a long time, Bud basked in the company of a bright, attractive woman. When the meal was over, he escorted her back to her car. Crossing the snowy street in front of the diner, he reached out to take her hand.

"Why, Sheriff, what a surprise!" she said.

"It's not really official," he said. "We're both wearing gloves."

It felt good to laugh.

CHAPTER TWENTY-ONE

Collecting Fees

Friday, December 3, 1976

Garrett Stilton could hardly see. He was already angry at the arrogant bastard who ordered him to St. Louis. By noon, light snow had turned to sleet. Ice clung to his windshield, the ragged wipers piling it up in great arcs where he most needed to see. Add to that his bald tires, and it was all he could do to keep the Lincoln on the highway.

He noticed the control tower for Lambert-St. Louis International passing by on his left like a ghost in the fog. He strained to find the exit for the road around the east end of the airport. Stilton rolled his window down to look for landmarks. The off-ramp exited on the right. It connected with a service road and led to a stoplight, where he had to make a left turn. Unable to stop on the ice, he slid across the intersection and bounced off the curb. He managed to negotiate the turn without hitting anyone. Next, he had to cross an overpass spanning the highway. The bridge was a sheet of ice. He spun his tires, burning his way up and over, and then fought to keep the car straight coming down the other side. When he finally got to the bottom, he could no longer see out. He had no choice. He was going to have to stop.

Stilton eased onto the right shoulder and parked beside a gravel turn-off. Clicking on his flashers, he swung the door wide open. Then he stepped out into the wind and sleet to clear the windshield. When he closed the door, his feet spun on the ice and he nearly fell. He clung to the car and shuffled forward until he could reach the wipers.

No gloves. No scarf. No scraper. He swore and pulled out his wallet. He rummaged through a handful of plastic cards. He picked one that was over the credit limit and used it to scrape the windows.

Stilton flinched as an airliner plunged out of the clouds toward him, wheels down, engines spooling up. He swore at the noisy giant as it cleared the fence and settled into a landing on the runway. He watched white vortices spiraling from the wingtips and flaps like smoke, trailing whizzing noises behind.

Only then did he realize he had stopped beside the ranks of strobe lights leading aircraft to the centerline of the runway. He swore at himself, the cold, the noise, his lousy car, and shook his hands to fling the wet snow off. Then he climbed back behind the steering wheel. He was late, and Mr. Bryce wouldn't be happy. It was enough to make him long for the courtroom again. He didn't go to court much these days because he wasn't very good at it. But at least it had kept him indoors.

Stilton's icy Lincoln crunched up to the main gate of Wheelan and Bryce Aerospace Corporation. He identified himself to the guard but found it irksome to sit shivering in the cold with the window down. He waited while the guard checked with Bryce's secretary. Once all the excuses were used up, the guard had no choice but to let him in. He gave Stilton a briefing about where to park. Then, just to be sure, he repeated himself word for word. Stilton's teeth chattered from the cold.

"Thank you. ..." he said, raising the window, "moron."

Deep snow and icy patches made the parking lot treacherous even for a person with a normal gait. By the time he battled his way to the building, his right shoe was full of slush. Snow stood piled on the toe. He stomped into the foyer, dislodging blobs of melting snow, and found himself standing before a marble desk. Behind it sat another guard. Apparently, these guys didn't talk to each other. He went through the whole explanation again. Stilton noticed that, aside from the man behind the desk, he was the only person in sight.

"Where is everybody?" he asked.

"Where have you been?" the guard asked. "Everybody went home. The airport is closed 'cause the weather is getting bad."

"Oh, great. You gonna tell me Mr. Bryce went home, too?"

The guard looked up and beyond Stilton.

"I assure you that is not the case," said a female voice behind him. "He might prefer to be home, but we waited for you. We will leave once your transaction is complete. Follow me, please."

Stilton had to sign in. The guard shoved a visitor's pass across the counter and motioned for him to clip it to his tie.

He found the ride up the elevator unnerving. The woman in the business suit ignored him all the way to the top floor. There was a hint of perfume in the air, but she stood motionless, her eyes fixed on the numbers over the door. It was like he wasn't even there. She came back to life when the bell rang and the door opened, and swiftly led him toward the end of the wing. Stilton saw her punch numbers into a keypad before stepping into a suite with floor-to-ceiling windows overlooking the airport.

"Right this way," she said as she led him through double doors made of frosted glass. Walter Bryce sat behind an enormous desk. He was a huge man, feet up, ankles crossed, his hands on top of his head, elbows out. Waiting.

"That will be all, thank you," he said without moving. The woman pulled the doors closed as she left.

"You've got some explaining to do," Bryce said. He didn't move. "So talk to me."

"You wanted it clean, so it is. No one can connect you. The stuff is in a bank box, and nobody knows anything," said Stilton.

"Don't come in here bullshitting me, Garrett. Someone had to pick up the package in DC. Someone had to haul it to Raleigh. Somebody made a pick-up at the airport, and somebody put it in the bank. I want to know every link in the chain. All of it. In case something happens to you. I want to know where it is, how it got there, and how to get it back without getting anything on me. So start."

Bryce didn't move. It made Stilton nervous. He started to fidget.

"Okay. I hired a courier service to pick up the satchel at the address you gave me," Stilton said. "Triple-A Couriers. I had them take it to the general aviation terminal and leave it at the fuel desk at Royer Aviation. I called the desk and gave them the tail number of the plane that would pick it up."

"Which was?"

"November five zero eight three two."

"Which is?"

"A Cessna 172."

"And the pilot?"

"A kid named Russell. A flight instructor who thinks he was on a charter."

Bryce took in a deep breath and let it out slowly.

"Right," said Bryce. "Kid gets a charter to fly a clunker from the boot-heel to DC, pick up a bag, fly it to Raleigh in the middle of the night, and toss it in the trash with some empty oil cans. A routine charter. Why should we trust him?"

"Because he'll do anything to log flight time. Not very choosey. He got caught trying to fly dope out of the Ozarks. I helped him out. Wants an airline job."

"I got news for you," growled Bryce.

"What's that?"

"That ain't gonna happen. We don't build planes for turds like that. End of story."

Walter Bryce finally took his hands off his head, put his feet on the floor, and leaned forward on the desk. He clasped his hands together and held Stilton in a steady gaze.

"Go on."

"Guy who picked the briefcase up is in the garbage business. Junior Petiole. He owes me. I get him out of jail when he needs it, and I keep him out of court. He does what I say."

"So what's in it for him?"

"He picks up the package and delivers it where I say, that's all."

"Which is?"

"Local dry cleaners. The guy has people wanting to sue him. I paid them off and told them to go away. He does me favors when I need."

"I'll bet. What's his name?"

"Clyde Dewey. Blue-Belle Cleaners. It's in the Yellow Pages."

Bryce stood, turned to look out the window, and shoved his hands in his pockets. He sighed and spoke without turning around.

"Jesus Christ, Stilton. Let me see if I got this right. You hired some wino to haul this shit across DC. You leave it unattended at a fifth-rate fixed-base operator. You let a drug runner fly it halfway across the country. You get a garbage collector to dump it in a trash can in an alley somewhere, and a damn dry cleaner takes it to the bank, singing 'Zippidy Doo-Dah.' Is that about right?"

"Well, not exactly," said Stilton. "See, it's all compartmentalized. Each guy only knows his little part of it. I'm the only one who knows the whole deal."

"You stupid son of a bitch. No, you're not. I know. And I don't like it."

Bryce hoisted up his pants, unselfconsciously unbuckling his belt to tighten it up another notch. Somehow, Stilton found the gesture intimidating.

"Wait a minute. I did what you asked, and did it fast," Stilton said. "Give me some credit, for God's sake."

Bryce stepped out from behind the desk and approached him. He stopped an arm's length away. Then he cupped one elbow in his hand and used his free hand to prop up his chin. He cocked his head slightly, as though trying to work out a puzzle.

"Follow my thinking on this, Stilton. Someone steps on the cleaner, and he says where he found the stuff. Step on the garbage guy, and he tells where he got it. Check flight plans and weather briefings, and you've got the plane and pilot. Ask the right question at National Airport, and you get the courier service. And I can damn well assure you they wrote down the address for the pick-up. Every single one of these people will turn around and point at you and say, 'He's the one who made me do it.' Can you see why I'm a little concerned here?"

"What the hell is the big problem? You said move it. I moved it. You said hide it where it's safe. I did. What is the big deal?"

Walter Bryce was peeved, and he made no effort to conceal it. He picked up his favorite paperweight, a piston from an old aircraft engine, and began rolling it back and forth between his hands.

"I'm not going to get into that with you. You don't need to know. But here's something you do need to know. If any one of these clowns goes flaky on us, I will personally cram your ass down a cannon and blast it through a running jet engine. Do you get my drift?"

"You make yourself clear," Stilton said. "But I did what you said. How about I just collect my fee and get out of here."

"The money will be in a satchel behind the right rear tire of your car. Don't back over it on your way out. You didn't expect me to cut you a check, did you?"

"No. Cash money is good. Can I leave now?" asked Stilton.

"By all means, please do. Just keep all your clowns inside the car."

Mr. Bryce's secretary entered on cue and opened the doors.

"Right this way, please."

Stilton followed her to the elevator, catching the same faint whiff of perfume. She ignored him in the elevator until the car landed at the ground floor. She led him to the security desk to surrender the visitor's tag, and then to the door. On her cue, the guard rose and came forward with a ring of keys to let Stilton out.

He stomped back out into the bitter cold and heard them lock the door behind him. He staggered off through the blizzard, swearing at the cold, about the guards, about that prissy broad, but most of all about that arrogant bastard in the penthouse.

When he got to his Lincoln he went around to the right rear tire. There, a satchel had been wedged behind the wheel and hastily covered with snow. He fought with it until he could get it free and went around to the driver's door, fumbling in his pocket for the key. By now his hands were so numb he had difficulty getting the key in the ignition.

Once he got the engine running and the heat turned up high, he switched on the dome light and pulled the satchel open. Only then did his spirits brighten.

Stilton's ordeal wasn't over. On his way back to Interstate 70, his car slid off into a ditch. Standing outside in the stinging sleet and snow, it didn't take him long to decide to abandon the car. The airport Marriott hotel was not far away. He grabbed the satchel and headed in that direction. A little after five thirty, he entered the lobby and stomped off the snow. His ears hurt and his hands were red and raw. He walked up to the registration desk.

"Yes, sir, how may I help you?" asked the attractive dark-skinned woman behind the counter.

"I need a room."

"We do have vacancies. How many nights will you be staying with us?" she asked.

"Until this storm is over and I can get my car out of the ditch," he said.

"Why don't we say three nights, and go from there?"

"Uh, yeah, sure. That will be fine," Stilton said.

"Will this be cash or credit card?"

"Cash," he said.

Those three days gave Stilton the time to hatch a plan. On the second day he telephoned a recent client. Less than a year earlier, Jeremy Bryce, son of Walter Bryce, had been picked up selling pot on campus in Raleigh. Stilton managed to bargain it down to simple possession. Walter Bryce had been much happier with him then.

"Jeremy, this is Garrett Stilton. How are you doing? Yeah, I know. I'm stranded, too, but it has given me some time to think. I have a nest egg, and I was wondering if you still have supply connections in Indianapolis."

Garrett listened carefully. He was looking for a way in. Jeremy Bryce could be it.

"Well, I don't know," he said. "Tell them you're going skiing in Colorado. Wait. Wait. Wait ... just think about this. I've got a pilot on the hook. He could get the stuff here overnight. There are like what, eight colleges in a thirty-mile radius? What could we do with a market of seventy, eighty thousand students?"

Stilton could hear Jeremy coming around.

"I don't know. Let's be reasonable. Say, run it up as far as it will go, and get out in like five years ... Indianapolis? Just as soon as I can get my car out of a ditch, I say we go. Okay. I'll call you. Let me write that down. This a girlfriend's number? Gotcha. I'll be in touch."

CHAPTER TWENTY-TWO

The Investigative Journalist

Thursday, March 17, 1977

It had been a hard winter. In some places snow drifted higher than Raymond's thighs. During his daily treks, he saw cattle dying in the fields. Very few cars traveled the rural roads. Raleigh County had dug in for the duration.

That was part of what drove him outside. He had the county to himself, and it was peaceful underneath a blanket of snow. When he got cold, he simply built a fire wherever he was. He had no schedule to keep. After warming himself, he would heap snow on the embers and move on. The wintry landscapes offered a tranquility he had not known in years.

During the weeks before when he had been trying to kill himself slowly with scotch, no one could reach him, not even Meredith. Then two things happened to break through his depression. A dog showed up. Raymond called him Tracker, short for Extraction. The two became inseparable. Tracker loved the snow.

The second was a visit he had from Millie during late January. In the hours before dawn, he had wandered down to the dock with a bottle of scotch in hand. He became too drunk to walk, so he watched the sunrise from the dock. He sat in an Adirondack chair and waited for daylight to clear his head.

The lake was still, the water the color of pewter. Fog hovered above it, and as the sunlight slid down the hill, it gradually burned the fog away. At daybreak, Raymond thought he heard Millie's voice calling to him across the water.

"Write, Raymond. Write or die," he heard her say.

Raymond was never certain whether it had been a dream. His head said it was a memory, but his heart said Millie was there. It was the same thing she told him years before when he was grieving for his lost army buddies. Because of her, he wrote *A Soldier's Heart*. Somewhere along the way, Raymond and Millie fell in love. In honoring those who had died, he became whole again.

He stayed on the dock as long as he could stand the cold, but he heard no more. Numb from frostbite, he finally went inside. He tried to make coffee, but his fingers felt like wood. He got water running in the sink and stuck his hands in. Soon, they felt like they were on fire.

He made coffee and tore open the drawers looking for a pen or pencil. He had no tablets, only paper bags from the Piggly-Wiggly. Hours later, he would realize he had cut his hands fumbling with his pen-knife. Words did not come easily. He just wrote what he wanted to say to Millie. It was the first of many love letters.

As Tracker put on weight, Raymond spent more sober days writing. The isolation of the harsh winter seemed to do him some good. He began making appearances in town, Tracker riding beside him in the pickup. By the middle of March, Raymond was weary of grieving and ready to get his life back. He went to the *Raleigh Journal-Messenger*.

"Lou, I'm not asking for a job. I'm just asking for a chance to write. I know there are things you can't pursue because you can't afford to put reporters on them. Let me take those assignments," he said.

"I'm not sure that is such a good idea," Lou said.

"There is no cost to you, and no risk. If my stuff isn't any good, you don't have to publish it. Since Millie's gone, I need a purpose. Otherwise, I'll wind up killing myself, just like the others."

Lou turned to stare out his office window, arms folded, his back to Raymond. Raymond recognized the time for silence. Eventually, the editor drew in a large breath and blew it out in exasperation. He turned to look Raymond in the eye, arms outspread.

"Raymond, I know you can write. I know you can do the work. But I have to think about the *Journal-Messenger*. That's where we have two problems."

"And those would be?"

"The first is your drinking. When folks see your byline, are they going to wonder whether you were drunk or sober when you wrote it?" Lou asked.

"Understood. That means the writing will have to answer for itself. What is the second?"

"Everyone in town knows Garrett Stilton filed a wrongful death lawsuit against Millie's estate, and they are going to wonder whose axe you are grinding," said Lou. "Besides, I can't let the paper get drawn into a lawsuit, either directly or indirectly."

Lou stood with his hands on his hips. Raymond pulled out a yellow envelope and offered it to him.

"Maybe this will help."

Lou hesitated. Raymond thrust it toward him.

"Go ahead," Raymond said. "Take it. Read it. Please."

Slowly, Lou reached for the envelope. He fished out a single sheet of paper folded in thirds. He unfolded it and read.

December 1, 1976

From: Garrett R. Stilton, Attorney at Law

To: Mr. Raymond Reginald Thornton

Re: Withdrawal of a complaint against the estate of Millicent Margaret (McKenna) Thornton

Dear Sir;

*Considering the forensic ambiguities regarding the
nature of Mr. Byron Donovan's death, and out of respect
for the memory of the recently deceased Mrs. Thornton,
the Stilton Law Firm has decided, for the present, to
withdraw our filing of a wrongful death lawsuit against
the estate of Mrs. Thornton. We have so notified the
district court.*

Yours truly,

Garrett R. Stilton

Garrett R. Stilton
Senior Partner
The Law Firm of Stilton & Associates

Raymond watched Lou take another deep breath and blow it out.

"Can we just take it one article at a time?" Raymond asked.

Lou finally softened.

"Okay. Story by story. But I'm not doing this for you. I'm doing this for Millie," he said.

Raymond held out his hand.

"That makes two of us, Lou."

Hesitantly, Lou shook hands with him.

"So, what do you want me to write about?" Raymond asked.

"I dunno. Go find something."

"You're a hard man, boss."

"Get out of here. I've got a paper to run."

"Yes, sir."

As Raymond left the office, he drew comfort from the familiar sights, sounds, and smells. The clatter of the linotype was still audible outside the building. He had one chance. It was all he needed. But he could sure use a big story.

CHAPTER TWENTY-THREE

Weed

Friday, March 25, 1977

Melanie saw the rig stop in front of the office door instead of entering the yard. She watched Harlan swing down and pull a bundle off the front seat. The metal door to the office swung open and he stepped inside.

"Hey, Harlan. What's up?" asked Melanie.

She put down her book and coffee mug. Harlan walked over to her desk and put the bundle on the corner.

"Junior dropped another bag of pot on my route today. This is the third time. I am tired of covering for him, and I sure don't need to blow my parole."

"What are you talking about?" she asked.

Melanie picked up the package and turned it over in her hands. She was caught off-guard.

"What did you say was in here?"

"That there's a two-kilo bag of grass. It was lying on top of the trash at the Gamma House. Junior is so damn dumb that he hasn't figured out that half his drops could wind up getting spread around out there," he said, thumbing in the direction of the landfill.

"Wait a minute, Harlan," Melanie said. "You need to break this down into small chunks for me. Is this why he has been yanking the Packmaster away from the regular routes?"

Harlan stood with his thumbs hooked in his pockets.

"Looks like it. He takes her out to make his drops. Nobody pays any attention. Except he delivers ahead of the runs sometimes. Sooner or later, one of the guys is gonna accidentally haul away the product. Then Junior's gonna get some customer backlash, and I don't want no part of it."

Melanie held up the bundle and twisted it in the air, pointing at it with the index finger of her other hand.

"You mean, like this customer right here might notice he's been ripped off?"

Harlan took off his cap and rubbed his head. Then he put it back on.

"I'm gonna take it back. I just brought it in to show you I'm not making shit up. So, what do we do about this?" he asked.

Melanie propped an elbow on the desk and planted her chin in her palm. She scowled and poked the bundle with one finger. Then she looked up at Harlan.

"Right now, you and me look like drug dealers. We could lose our city contract over something like this. And we sure as hell don't need your parole officer to walk in. Let me think about this. When do you plan to put it back?" she asked.

Harlan thought about that for a moment.

"I can get it on my last load. Swing by the dumpster and toss it in before I bring the truck in for the day," he said.

"That's a plan," Melanie said.

Harlan shifted his weight. He looked at the bundle. Then he looked Melanie in the eye.

"You want a suggestion?" he asked.

"Whatcha thinking?"

"Call the sheriff on this one. Handle it straight up. Ain't none of us here needs to get caught up in Junior's mess."

"You're making sense, Harlan. I wasn't ready for that," Melanie said.

"Just don't stall too long, lady. Junior could come back any time."

He turned to go out the door without another word. Melanie was all alone, staring at a bundle that would decide her future. She needed to make the right decision.

Harlan dumped his load and headed back out on his route before the sheriff arrived. Melanie spotted Bud coming down the drive. He parked close to the office door. He took a moment to do a visual 360. Melanie figured all he would see was a dozer working fifty yards away shoving garbage into the landfill, her rusty Ford, and the old Dodge that belonged to the guy on the dozer. Moments later, the door opened and the sheriff stepped in.

"Hey, Bud," she said.

"Melanie, how you doin'?"

She straightened her desk pad with one finger.

"We got a problem."

"Who's we?"

"You, me, the company, Grandpa, our drivers, but especially Junior."

Bud took off his hat and wiped his forehead with a handkerchief.

"Keep going."

"Harlan brought this in," she said, reaching down between her ankles to pick up the package. She held it out to the sheriff.

"What have we got here?" Bud asked.

"This is what Junior has been doing. He uses the Packmaster to make special deliveries. Except he sometimes gets there before the other men make their rounds. Harlan found this in the dumpster at the Gamma House. If he hadn't looked in first, we might be spreading it around down the hill right now. Harlan doesn't want to bust parole, so he brought this in to prove he wasn't bullshitting me."

Bud cocked an eyebrow.

"He thought nobody would miss it?"

"He knows damn well it will be missed. He plans to take it back on his last run today. I figured you would know what we should do here better than anyone."

Bud crossed his arms while he considered that. It didn't take him long to make a decision.

"Okay. Let me get the camera. Be right back," he said.

Bud brought in an evidence kit and a 35mm Nikon. Melanie was standing by the window keeping watch. He decided it was a good idea.

Bud quickly placed the bundle on the corner of Melanie's desk and took photos. Then he weighed it with a portable scale. Two kilograms. Then he sliced open the package at one corner and took out a small sample and weighed it. He snapped photos at each step. He put the sample in a plastic evidence bag before writing down the time, date, and location. Then he placed it in his evidence kit.

"Okay, so who does this weed belong to?" he said, taping up the small hole.

"Some college kid at the Gamma House, I guess. Figured you might want to see who retrieves it."

She stood, arms folded, swaying back and forth nervously.

"Melanie, you are something else. We may have time to get the Gamma House under surveillance. This is quite a case you've opened up here. But I have to get more than Junior and a local dealer off the streets. I want the whole network. You and Harlan have a problem with that?"

"Harlan will be fine with it. He wants to stay clean, so he will cooperate. Not a word to his parole officer, okay?"

"Not about this. He's helping us. Let me get out of here. Call me when Harlan starts his last run."

"Okay. Thanks. Hey, Bud ... do you think this could be the end for Junior?"

There was desperation in her voice.

"It's too early to tell. We need to convict him, not just piss him off. I'll try to keep you out of it."

Melanie took in a deep breath and let it out slowly.

"Well, I gotta tell you something."

"What?"

"If you don't do it soon, I'll have to. I'm starting to run out of rope."

Bud froze and focused all his attention on her.

"I'm guessing there's more to that," he said.

Melanie looked down at the floor and kicked at something she saw there.

"He keeps threatening to kill me."

"Easy, Melanie. Tell me what's been going on."

She hugged herself and swayed back and forth, revealing just how big this was to her.

"You ever had a forty-four held under your nose?"

Bud flinched.

"No. Can't say that I have."

"It gets kinda personal."

Bud put everything down and looked at her.

"Melanie, has it really gone that far?" he asked.

"Oh, yeah. But he is never gonna do it again."

Her voice had an edge.

"Why not?"

Melanie pointed one finger at him like a gun and looked Bud squarely in the eye.

"Because I'm not gonna give him another chance."

Melanie had drawn her line in the dirt. Sheriff Bud needed to understand that.

Bud took off his hat and ran his fingers through his hair. Then he put it back on and tugged it into place.

"Melanie, you need to go away for a while. Be safe. Take some time off."

She locked her eyes on him. Bud had to get this message.

"I'm not leaving. Everyone is at his mercy. He is dangerous. Pardon the expression, but I'm the only one around here with the balls to stand up to him."

"He has always been dangerous. So what else is new?"

Melanie leaned on her fists on her desk and glared at the sheriff.

"I'm not joking. He could pull this whole company down with him. Guys like Harlan need a break, not another turn in the big house. Junior's messing with a whole lot of lives here, and I can't stand by and let him screw us all."

Bud held out both palms.

"I'll get him, Melanie. I just have to do it by the book."

Melanie gave him one last chance.

"You've got your book. I got mine. You get first crack at him, but you need to know that yours is not the only clock ticking."

Bud's eyebrows rose. He picked up his camera and evidence kit.

"I got the message. Tell Harlan we'll be taking pictures. Tell him not to freak," said Bud.

"I'll babysit Harlan. You go do your job. But do it quickly."

"It's gonna take time, Melanie."

Melanie's eyes narrowed.

"Why?"

Bud turned to point at the bundle on her desk.

"Well, right now, I can't put those two kilos in Junior's hands. The judge won't go for it if all I can say is, 'Your Honor, we just *know* it came from him.' Even a bad lawyer will catch on. We have to track a shipment from the plane into Junior's possession, watch him make a drop, and wait for the buyer to pick it up. Only then can we make an arrest."

Melanie sat down heavily in her chair and scowled.

"I don't like it," she said drumming her fingers on the desk.

He opened the door.

"I know. I don't either. See you."

"Okay."

Melanie heard the dozer clanking away in the distance. She placed the telephone handset on her shoulder while she dialed the old man. As the phone rang, she pulled the bundle off the top of her desk and placed it on the floor by her feet. He answered on the second ring. She could hear a TV game show in the background.

"Hey, Pops. How ya doing?"

"How come I don't like calls from you that start out that way?" Old Man Petiole snarled.

She rummaged through her desk for some chewing gum.

"Cause you know I never call unless it's important."

"Shit."

"You can say that again."

She found two sticks and started unwrapping them while holding the phone to her ear with her shoulder.

"What is it this time? Junior in jail again?"

"Not yet, but I got something here at the office you need to see."

She folded the gum into her mouth.

"What's the matter? You can't just come right out and tell me? I gotta drive down there to see for myself?"

She kept her eyes on the window and decided it was time to move things along.

"I got a bag of dope Junior hid in a trash can," she said. "Sheriff says two kilos. Harlan thinks Junior's dealing out of the truck."

"Wait a minute. Hold on. The sheriff was there? He's seen it?"

Now the old man was getting the picture. Melanie relaxed into her seat. She rocked and watched the road.

"Yeah. It's like an open house today. He just left. We still got punch and cookies. Whaddya think—can you spare a couple of minutes?"

"I'm on my way. Don't do nothing until I get there."

Melanie ignored the old man's instruction. She'd been thinking about it for a while. She pulled a pair of scissors out of her desk and waddled into the store room. There she opened a storage cabinet and removed a green box of rat poison. She carried it into Junior's office and searched until she found a fifth of Jack Daniels hidden between his desk and the wall.

She unscrewed the cap from the bottle and then cut a corner off the box. She carefully poured the contents into the bourbon. Then she replaced the cap and swirled the bottle around to dissolve the poison.

A minute later, she wiped the bottle down, put it back, blew the desk clean, and returned to the front office with the crumpled green box in her hand. She stepped outside and threw it onto the roof of the building. As she stepped back inside, she felt ecstatic. Pops would get there any minute, but he didn't have to know everything.

Just as Melanie expected, when Old Man Petiole saw the parcel, he was furious.

"I'm gonna have to fire my own son," he ranted. "Except I can't do it right now. If I bust up the sheriff's investigation, I will have real problems."

Melanie could tell he was pissed off.

"All right," the old man said. "You give Bud Oswald whatever he needs to catch him in the act, and the sooner the better."

Melanie blew bubbles and tried to conceal how pleased she was that the old man had had enough.

"You can count on me, Pops."

Old Man Petiole stormed off in a rage.

Melanie knew it could take weeks, so she kept dosing Junior's bourbon. Every time he broke the seal on a new bottle, she gave it the treatment. After the fifth box lodged on the roof, she began to notice the effects. Bruises appeared on Junior's hands and arms, not the deep blue-green kind, but bright purple blotches, just under the skin, the color of eggplant.

CHAPTER TWENTY-FOUR

Foul Play

Thursday, March 31, 1977

About ten minutes after nine at night Junior left Cozy's bar just drunk enough to go rob the dry cleaner. He had figured out who was handling the money and convinced himself he wasn't getting his fair share. He launched his '74 Montego over the curbstones and headed to town. The ride was bumpier than he remembered.

When Junior tried the back door of the dry cleaning shop, he found it unlocked. He stepped in and looked around, but saw no one. He was too far gone to wonder why the lights were on. He found the little office and sat down in the chair to start ransacking the desk. That's what he was doing when Clyde tip-toed in, push-broom raised high overhead, and swung at the intruder's head with all his might. Junior saw shadows moving on the wall and turned to look. The blow missed its mark.

Junior caught the handle of the broom with full force across his right shoulder. The handle snapped in two, the brush ricocheting off into the corner. Junior bellowed in pain and started to rise, clumsily pulling his gun from his shoulder holster, his right arm and hand still crippled with pain. Junior lunged at Clyde.

Suddenly Junior felt an excruciating pain in his belly. The smaller man had stopped him the only way he could. Junior looked down to see the broom handle protruding from his belly. Eyes wide with fear, he watched Clyde give it a second lunge to drive it home. Junior stumbled back in horror at the bloody wood sticking out of his gut. He tried to talk but could not. He dropped the gun on the floor, grabbed the wood protruding from his abdomen, and tried to pull it out. It wouldn't budge.

Clyde scooped the gun up off the floor and stuck it in Junior's face with a shaky hand.

"Get out," he said, and motioned Junior to the door. Junior tried to talk again, but only gurgling noises came out. He braced himself against the wall with a bloodied hand and began to make his way outside.

"Ahhhh … God damn … it … hurts!" Junior bellowed.

The smaller man kept waving the gun.

"You want to get shot in the head? Keep moving," Clyde warned.

"Unhhh … leaving … can I have … my gun? Keep the bullets. Just gimme … back my gun."

"What, do you think I'm crazy?"

"Latch … on the handle … ejects."

Junior leaned against the wall, watching Clyde step away, fumbling with the gun until the cylinder jumped out of the latch. He swung it open and discovered the ejector rod. The dry cleaner pumped it until the last round fell on the floor. Then he shoved the door open wide and hurled the gun out into the alley.

"You want it, go get it," Clyde yelled.

Junior reeled out the door, searching for his beloved Smith and Wesson. Junior couldn't get a grip on the broom handle because it was slick with his own blood. He found his gun, climbed into the front seat of his car, closed the door, and then started the engine. He sat dazed, trying to figure out where to go next.

Someone tapped on the glass. Relieved to get some help, Junior rolled the window down. A dark figure stuck a gun in his face and said, "You Junior Petiole?"

"Unh huh."

"Scoot over. We're going for a ride."

Junior was weak with shock and pain.

"Who the hell are you?" he grunted. "What do you mean a ride?"

He felt a second gun press against the back of his neck. A new voice spoke from behind him.

"Do what the man said."

Junior scooted. He was fading fast.

"In case you haven't noticed, I got a broom handle sticking out of my guts. It hasn't been a very good night for me, so maybe you boys can come back in a couple of days."

"Don't think so. Word has it that you been ripping off the shipments. Only one way I know to fix that. So shut up and enjoy your last few minutes in peace."

Junior passed out and slumped against the window.

Later, when he came to his senses again, they were arguing. Junior played possum.

"Let's just do him and get out of here."

"No point in making noise. Let's just sit here and watch him die."

"Could take hours. I say lets do what we came here to do."

"Inside the car?"

"Naw. Too messy. Let's get him outside so we can make sure he's dead."

As the men exited the car, Junior slid his gun out of his holster and held his hand near his belly. His car door opened, and one of the guys reached in to grab him under the arms. Junior slapped him across the bridge of his nose with the gun. Kicking the door into the second guy, he clambered out and began pistol whipping them both. His rage was there, but he didn't have much power left. One of the guys kicked him hard in the broom handle. It was all over. Junior went down in a heap.

"C'mon, let's get outta here."

"You stupid sumbitch. Take a good look around. You live in a dump; now you're gonna die in a dump."

The two men got into Junior's car and drove away.

He looked around. Even in total darkness he could tell from the smell where he was. Junior slowly pushed himself up to a sitting position. He felt around his belly and discovered that he was bleeding

117

profusely. He had no choice. Somehow he had to get inside the office to call an ambulance.

He tried to get up, but he couldn't get his legs under him. He rocked onto his back to rest. Then he heard a familiar sound in the distance.

The dozer started up. Then it began clanking toward him in the darkness.

"Who's there? What are you doing?" called Junior.

No one answered. He strained to see in the darkness. He thought he could make out the looming shape of the dozer coming toward him.

"What the hell's going on here? I'm hurt. I need help," he called out.

This time he got an answer. A familiar voice called to him over the clatter of the steel tracks.

"I'm gonna take care of all that."

Junior felt a rush of relief.

"Who is that? Pops, is that you?" Junior cried.

The bulldozer kept coming.

"Hush now. There's no call for yelling," came the reply.

"Oh, thank God you showed up. I'm in a pretty bad way here."

"Just relax. This won't take long," said his father over the clanking steel tracks.

CHAPTER TWENTY-FIVE

The Call

Friday, April 1, 1977

The phone call to the sheriff's office came in at 7:32 AM. Sam Whiteside covered the mouthpiece with his hands and swiveled around to pass the message to Bud.

"Sheriff, we got a problem."

"What is it?"

"Junior has gone and got himself under a bulldozer."

"Say again?"

"Caterpillar. D-3. You need to go out to the city dump."

"Okay. Show me enroute. As soon as the next deputy walks in the door, you come out to help me. Bring cameras and an evidence kit. I think I'd better get out there pronto."

Actually, there was no need to hurry.

By the time Bud got to the scene, the driveway between the blacktop and the dump was lined with cars. When he drove up to the gate, Melanie, dressed in a denim shift and a yellow sweater, was waiting. When he approached, she swung it open for him. He pulled in and parked his truck just inside. Melanie closed the gate behind him and walked over. He rolled down the window.

"Who found him?" Bud asked.

"Harlan. He was the first one to arrive. He went out to see why the dozer was parked over there. Once he saw what was out there, he used his car to block the gate to keep everyone out. Then he called me."

"Who else has been inside the gate this morning?"

"Only Harlan. He was so pale and shaky. He told us not to go out there."

"Good. So Harlan identified Junior?"

"Yup. And that's good enough for me. I don't want to see what he described."

"I do understand," Bud said.

"Do you think I should shut down for the day? Send everybody home?"

"Right now, the only two I need to talk to are you and Harlan. Go ahead and send all the others home. But until further notice, this whole area is a crime scene," Bud said. "That means no one comes in here unless I say so, okay?"

"Got it."

Melanie nodded toward the office building.

"Any problem if me and Harlan wait inside?"

"That depends. Can you stay off the phones?" he asked. "Folks in this town can start rumors faster than we can collect evidence."

"No calls. Promise."

"Okay. Send everybody home now and go on inside, but ask Harlan to come out to see me."

"Sure thing."

Harlan looked pale and on the verge of losing his breakfast. Bud asked him to point out the path he walked on his way to the dozer. It was pretty much a straight line from the front porch to the dozer and back. Then he asked to see his shoe soles. Harlan lifted his Redwing boots. After that Bud sent him inside.

As the employees started driving off, Bud took a deep breath and prepared himself. He walked the perimeter of the parking lot until he was on the landfill side of the scene. Then he moved in slowly, checking the ground in front of every step. He didn't want to destroy any evidence, but it was difficult because he was walking across a garbage dump.

When Sam Whiteside arrived, Bud stopped where he was. Sam collected all his gear. Bud circled his hand in the air to show him which way to enter the scene to come in behind him.

When Sam caught up with him, Bud filled him in on what little he knew. They walked into the crime scene totally unprepared. There was a lot of blood. The left track of the dozer had run up Junior's legs, stopping just short of the pelvis. Bloody handprints on the cleats of the track bore mute testimony to Junior's last fight.

His eyes and mouth were wide open in mid-scream; his right hand curled tightly around something protruding from his belly. Sam bent over and threw up.

"Okay, Sam. Give me the camera and go call the medical examiner. I'll start documenting the scene. When you get back, we'll try to see how he got out here."

Sam, who was very pale, seemed happy to go for a walk.

CHAPTER TWENTY-SIX

Hidden Evidence

Sunday, April 3, 1977

Melanie drove her rusty old Ford out to the dump while the sun was still below the horizon. She had a few details to clean up, and she needed the place all to herself.

She pulled to a stop in front of the gates, her headlights on the rusty chain and padlock. She often wondered why they installed gates at the dump in the first place. It wasn't like people would break in to steal stuff. Maybe the idea was to keep people from throwing trash away without permission. It always seemed ironic to her, but she never got around to asking.

She reached into her jacket pocket for a silver key. She clambered out of the car and walked over to the lock. It was stubborn as usual, so she spit on both sides of the key and jiggled it in the slot to loosen the tumblers.

When the hasp sprang free, the chain rattled to the ground. She gave a hefty shove on one arm of the gate. Rusty hinges complained as the welded iron pipe swung 180 degrees and banged into the chain link fence. Everything seemed loud this morning.

She drove her car into the lot, keeping well away from the bulldozer and the crime-scene tape. She parked out of sight of the road. Then she walked back to close the gate and drape the chain around the poles to make it appear the place was closed.

Getting rid of the Jack Daniels would be easy. She unlocked the office door and left it open to let in the light of dawn. Electric lights might draw unwanted attention. She walked straight into Junior's office to retrieve the bottle hidden between his desk and the wall. Then she went for a hike.

On her way out to the landfill, she had to smile. It had been so easy. She had asked Bud if she and Harlan could wait in the office. It was subtle, but it excluded the office from the crime scene.

Bud and that deputy were preoccupied with Junior's horrific death a hundred feet from the building. Because Harlan had been with her, she did not hide or move anything. That's why she was back today.

Melanie reached the edge of the excavation. Then she opened the bottle of Jack Daniels and poured the contents out on the ground. Grabbing the bottle by the neck, she lobbed it eighty feet or so out into the middle of the garbage heap. She heard it break when it hit.

She stood there for a moment searching her mind for things she might have missed. Then, snapping her fingers, she remembered all the empty bottles in the office trash cans. They still had small amounts of bourbon in them that could provide trace evidence. She headed back toward the building, hesitating by her car only long enough to pop the trunk.

Then she went room by room through the office, rummaging through every trash can to find all the empty liquor bottles. She filled Junior's wastebasket with bottles and hauled them all out to her car. Then she drove out to the landfill.

One at a time, she lobbed the empty bottles, each in a separate direction, into the pit. When she finished tossing the last one, she stood with her hands on her hips and stared out into the pile of trash. She asked herself again what she might have overlooked. She glanced down at tiny rivulets of bourbon inside the waste basket. Without hesitation, she tipped it over and stepped down on it until it caved in. Then she kicked it off into the hole as well.

Daylight had come, and Melanie could think of only one more thing that needed to be done. She hated ladders but didn't have much choice. She drove back to the office and pulled the extension ladder out of the store room. In the end, she chose the concrete pad in front of the door as the most stable platform. She didn't like the idea of falling onto the concrete step, but she also knew that when one leg of a ladder sinks into soft ground it guarantees a fall.

Climbing the ladder was the easy part. Shifting her bulk over the ledge and onto the flat roof was the scary part, especially without dumping the ladder. Just as she was stepping down off the ledge onto the roof, she heard traffic on the blacktop. She was caught midstride and unable to duck. Instead, she turned her face away from the road and froze.

She was perspiring now, dreading the sound of tires turning off the blacktop onto gravel. She imagined the worst case scenario. If Bud discovered she had tricked him, he would come to turn the office inside out. The sound of tires grew closer and closer. And then it passed. She let out a sigh when a truckload of hogs disappeared over the hill.

She wanted to rush around to pick up the empty boxes but forced herself to move slowly and deliberately. A lady her size must test the roof for soft spots before putting her full weight anywhere. She searched the roof methodically, finding six boxes. That seemed about right. She jammed them into her jacket pockets and returned to the ladder.

This was why she hated ladders. Down. She hated down. Especially looking down. So she sat on the ledge and swung her feet around to the outside. She kept her eyes on the horizon and scooted to her left, little by little, until she was touching the ladder. Then she searched with her left heel for a rung, got her footing, and carefully stood, her back to the ladder. Ever so deliberately, she began to turn her body until she could hold onto the rails and get her right toe on the rung. Concentrating for all she was worth, she balanced nearly four hundred pounds on her right big toe in order to twist her left foot around. She finally got both feet facing the same direction. Without looking down, she began to descend the ladder. One rung early, she stepped off the ladder and fell on her butt. The ladder slid off the roof and slammed across her leg.

When she got up and brushed herself off, she took inventory. Except for some bruises and a nasty abrasion across her shin, she was unhurt. She blew hair out of her sweaty face and resolved never to do that again.

For the last time today, Melanie marched to the edge of the excavation. She threw the empty boxes of rat poison to the winds. She was pretty sure Sheriff Bud was not going to tape off the whole landfill to search for evidence. Besides, dumps had rat poison for a reason. She hiked back to the office to lock up. Then she got in her car and went home.

CHAPTER TWENTY-SEVEN

Preparations

Sunday, April 3, 1977

Back at the sheriff's office, Bud gathered his best minds to go over the evidence for a joint briefing of the Raleigh Police Department and the sheriff's deputies on Monday morning. On hand were Lucy, Sam, and Deputy Cassius Greene. Cassius was a Vietnam veteran. His mind worked as hard as his body, and he was big, black, and buff.

Bud encouraged his people to challenge each other's thinking. It wasn't malice; it was due diligence.

"So it looks like Junior got speared somewhere else and then transported to the dump by person or persons unknown. Somebody pinned him down with the dozer and then left him to die and took off," said Sam.

Cassius spoke up.

"Now wait a minute. Something about that makes no sense."

"It's Occam's Razor," answered Sam. "The simplest answer is usually the correct answer."

"I'm with you on that, but according to what you just said, Junior is walking around with a spear in him. Somebody puts an arm around his shoulder and says, 'Hey, old buddy, let's go out to the dump for a while.' Junior says, 'Sure, okay, fine with me,' and they go to a place nowhere near a hospital. Then the guy says, 'Hey, Junior, you stay right here while I go get the bulldozer, which goes like three miles an hour, so's I can run it over you.' Man, there ain't no way that's simple."

They thought about what Cassius said for a moment.

"So Junior didn't go willingly," offered Lucy. "He was taken there by force. Any rope marks on his wrists or arms?"

"No ligature marks anywhere," answered Bud. "But that brings up an interesting point. The ME noticed numerous ..." Bud searched the table for a piece of paper, "'subcutaneous hematomas' on his extremities. Pools of blood beneath the skin. They were purplish in color, like hemorrhages. He said they reminded him of the bruising old people get who are on blood thinners. Doctors watch them because they can become bleeders. The ME is going to do some more tests. Incidentally, Junior's blood alcohol was .019 percent or better."

"Baseline for him," said Sam. "So what, exactly, is the cause of death here?"

Bud tapped on an eight-by-ten glossy showing the pool of blood at the scene.

"Exsanguination. Junior bled out right there," Bud answered.

"So, we are looking at a homicide, right?" asked Sam.

Cassius swept his hand over the photos spread out over the table.

"Unless Junior stabbed hisself, hitched a ride to the dump, and jumped under a dozer that just happened to be running at night, I'd say suicide is off the table."

"Very perceptive, Cassius. You have a way with words," Lucy said.

"Thank you." His smile lit up the room.

Bud turned to Cassius.

"So, what do you think about this being an accidental death?"

"Bud," he said, "I can't figure out how damn dumb you would have to be to get this done to yourself accidentally."

"So who killed Junior?" Sam asked.

Cassius decided to needle Sam.

"Occam's Razor says he cut himself shaving and died of natural causes," he said.

That did it. Lucy jumped in.

"I buy the bit about natural causes, because Lucy's Razor says if you're gonna get run through with a wooden stick and run over by a bulldozer, you are naturally gonna die."

Sam turned to Bud in exasperation.

"Sheriff," he said, "you lost control of this meeting, didn't you?"

"Yes. So let's figure out what we don't know, and then figure out how to get it."

"We need the car," Cassius said.

"You're right. That would tell us a lot," said Bud.

"We need a list of everyone at the dump who knows how to operate the bulldozer," said Sam.

"We also need to know the caliber of the stick," Lucy added.

She tried to keep a straight face.

"Thank you for your contribution," Bud said. "Perhaps it will be in the autopsy report."

They worked as a team of equals long into the night. When they left, the blackboard held a detailed chart of what they knew, a prioritized list of things they needed to know, and a plan to start moving them across the board. In the morning, every member of the sheriff's department and the Raleigh Police Department would hear the details.

One other person had been invited to that meeting: Raymond Thornton. Part of the plan was to decide what to keep out of the paper for now and how to use Raymond's articles to get the public to help.

CHAPTER TWENTY-EIGHT

Joining Forces

Monday, April 4, 1977

Bud let Al Jennings, the chief of police, enter the room first. Inside, eight uniformed police officers and two detectives from the Raleigh PD sat crammed together with six deputies, one dispatcher, and one very self-conscious investigative reporter. Bud studied the room. According to the script he and Chief Jennings had worked out that morning, Chief Jennings would begin.

"Let me start by addressing the members of my department. The sheriff has uncovered evidence of a dope ring in Raleigh. An informant produced a two-kilo bag of pot. Bud took samples and put it back in the dumpster at the Gamma House. They set up surveillance to see who came to get it."

Bud waited. He and the chief knew what was coming. A young cop near the front raised his hand. Jennings acknowledged him.

"Excuse me, chief. Isn't that in our jurisdiction?"

A squabble broke out in the corner, and then it spread. Soon everyone had something to say. Bud and Al let it go until it looked like fistfights were about to break out. That's when Jennings slammed his clipboard on the podium. It sounded like a gunshot. Every head in the room turned to look at him.

"Am I the only one who sees a problem here?" he said. "Everyone sit down and shut up so we can go through this thing."

He waited for the noise from shuffling feet and scraping chairs to subside.

The chief looked directly at the cop who asked the question.

"The deputies didn't bust anyone. They were following a county case. They believe the merchandise is coming in through the airport. That's outside the city limits. Bud saw the bag at the city dump. Again, outside the city limits. Now there's a homicide involved. Outside the city limits. Since the city of Raleigh lies entirely within the county, that means this is their turf, too. They have come to us for help, and I intend to provide it. So, just what is the nature of your objection?"

The young cop's face flushed. He was thinking as fast as he could.

"Uh, sir, I have no objection. I believe they should be commended for coming to the right place."

Bud smiled. Laughter and catcalls always made for a better working climate. When the noise died down again, the chief handed the meeting over to Bud.

Bud flipped a switch on the wall. Like a curtain rising in a play, a projection screen rose into a box near the ceiling. Behind it, the blackboard was full of information. Bud asked Sam to take everyone through the drug surveillance.

"Yeah, okay, here we go. March 25, Bud gets a call from Melanie Griggs at the city dump. A driver finds a bag of pot stashed in the dumpster behind the frat house. He says Junior is using a company truck to make deliveries. We set up to see who claims it.

"A kid drives up in a '70 Mustang Cobra, green with white stripes, gets out, and opens the trunk. He takes out a net on a pole and scoops up the bag of grass. He tosses it in the trunk and drives off. We got it on film. Missouri plate number 1AH-12W, registered to Jeremy Bryce, age twenty-two. For those of you who may not recognize the name, he is the son of Walter Bryce, president of Wheelan and Bryce Aerospace.

"He got busted last August for dealing, reduced to simple possession. Our photos jibe with his driver's license photo. Preppie-looking kid, penny loafers, no socks, khaki slacks, green and white sweater, close-cropped hair, and a baby mustache.

"New subject. Does it seem strange to you that the dry-cleaning business would be booming in Raleigh? Sheriff Bud overheard two bankers wondering why Clyde Dewey's deposits are way up. So here's what we think. We think Jeremy Bryce is dealing. Again. We think Clyde Dewey is the banker. We think Junior was a mule, but maybe his work ethic didn't measure up. So who can connect the dots? Bryce, Dewey, and Petiole. What do they have in common?"

The room fell silent while everyone tried to put it together.

"Let me give you a hint," Sam said. "Jeremy Bryce's lawyer was Tiltin' Stilton. Who kept Junior Petiole out of jail?"

Over a chorus of groans, several voices said, "Tiltin' Stilton."

Sam tapped his pencil three times on the podium and reached out like choir director.

"Okay now, class. Guess who Clyde Dewey's lawyer is."

He made an exaggerated downbeat.

"Tiltin' Stilton," came the chorus.

"Man! You guys are good!"

The room filled with laughter and side conversations. Sam sat down. Bud made eye contact with Chief Jennings, who gave a slight nod of his head. The message was clear. Let them talk.

Bud studied his audience. He finally saw deputies and cops talking, comparing notes, sharing ideas. Everyone was relaxed and focused. After a minute or two, he stepped to the podium and waited. The talking died down.

"Here is what we know about the murder of Junior Petiole," he started.

Instantly a hush fell over the room.

"Junior Petiole was a bleeder because he was full of brodifacoum, the primary agent used in rat poison. Mice and rats developed a tolerance for warfarin, so this stuff is two hundred times stronger.

"His levels were high enough to be lethal, but somebody killed him first. His blood wouldn't coagulate. We're gonna have a hard time figuring out who did it. Here's how it stacks up. He gets poisoned. Then he gets speared. Then somebody parks a D-3 Cat on him."

That was a conversation starter.

"Man, how many times can you get killed in one night?" someone asked from the back of the room.

"He musta run out of friends," said another.

"Naw, what he ran out of was blood."

Bud let them talk for a bit before he continued.

"He was impaled on a wooden shaft fifteen-sixteenths of an inch thick and about twenty-one inches long. The wood split along the grain, leaving a sharp point at the break.

"Oddly enough, Clyde Dewey, of dry cleaning fame, bought a new broom handle Saturday morning at Ace Hardware. Not a broom, mind you, just a handle. Deputy Green asked the guy at the store to measure one. Diameter was fifteen-sixteenths of an inch. According to our local authority on broom ballistics," he said, looking at Lucy, "that's a 23.8 mm weapon."

She took some heat. Then Bud finished up.

"The RPD and the sheriff's office are going partners on this. Detective Kuhlmann and Deputy Whiteside will command the operation. They will be like Siamese twins until this thing is over. Their decisions can be no better than the information they have to work with. That means the best source of ideas will be you guys out on the street. Cops with eyes on the suspects will see opportunities others might miss.

"If you and you partner think you have a good idea, call it in straight to Kuhlmann or Whiteside. If you take time to pass it up the chain of command we might miss an opportunity. Their job is to have the big picture. If they choose not to act, it is because they found a better option. Think about it from their point of view. It is always easier to choose between lots of good suggestions than to try to think of everything yourself. Does that make sense?"

Heads nodded, several voicing their agreement. Everyone in the room was paying attention.

"Any suggestions at this point?"

A hand went up in the front row.

"How will we know when the next shipment is coming?"

"Al and I talked about that. If we knew the point of departure, we could ask for help from Flight Service or Air Traffic, but we don't have that information yet. That leaves only one alternative. We'll have to place a team at the airport each night until the plane comes in. They scramble the rest of us when it arrives. Then they get what they can on the plane and pilot without blowing cover, and we use the time between the drop and the pickup to get in position. It's not perfect, but only two guys are up all night. We'll rotate teams between our department and yours until we hit bingo."

An officer in the back of the room stood until he was recognized.

"Yes, do we have another suggestion?"

"Yes, sir. Would a wire tap on Dewey put us onto on the next delivery?"

"Good question. Yes, it might. But all we have on him right now is suspicion. That gets us into unreasonable-search-and-seizure issues. Frankly, I don't think we can convince a judge that we have probable cause. What do you think?"

"Maybe while we are watching him, we can pick up something that would convince a judge to approve a tap."

"There you go. Good idea. Meanwhile, nothing keeps us from looking at his phone records, right? Maybe what the judge needs is in there. Let's get on that one right away. Thanks."

After fielding a few more questions, Bud brought the briefing to a close. Raymond and a couple others bolted for the door. Most hung back, talking and thinking about the case.

One of them was Al Jennings.

"You know, Bud, in my world, the brightest guys wind up detectives and work in a closed shop. But you give the beat cops a chance to play detective. Where did that notion come from?"

"To tell you the truth, it was an experiment. We wondered if we could outsmart the bad guys with a collective IQ. So far, we've had good results."

"Peculiar," said Jennings. "I guess we'll see if it works."

CHAPTER TWENTY-NINE

Filling In

Thursday, April 7, 1977

Raleigh Journal-Messenger

Man Found Dead at Landfill

By Raymond Thornton, Contributing Editor

> *The sheriff's department received a call early on the morning of April 1 reporting a body discovered at the municipal landfill. Because of the date, they thought at first it was a prank. Sheriff Bud Oswald responded to the scene and the case is now under investigation. The victim has been identified as Everett W. Petiole Jr., last seen leaving Cozy's Bar and Grill shortly after 9:00 PM on March 31.*

Stilton looked at Jeremy Bryce in disbelief. He was acting like a scared rabbit. He had no business coming to the office in the first place, let alone slamming a newspaper down on the desk. The kid stood there red-faced, huffing and puffing. He must have run all the way. Why not just put a sign on your back that says "Up to No Good"? Stilton put the cap on his pen and picked up the paper.

He rocked back in his chair and glanced at the article. Then he tossed it into the trash.

"Calm down," he said. "All we need to do is to make one little adjustment. For now, you gotta make the pickups and drops."

"You've gotta be crazy! We can't just keep on going after somebody gets killed like this," Jeremy yelled.

Stilton saw flecks of spittle on the boy's mouth. That called for a different strategy.

"Remember, now we get a bigger percentage, you and me. Junior was weak, but now he's gone," Stilton said. He used his most calm, reassuring tone. He called it his lawyer voice.

"This is a good thing for us, Jeremy, a really good thing. Orders are rolling in, and your project is working out well."

He watched the kid settle down a bit, trying now to become reasonable and persuasive. But he was still wringing his hands.

"I'm just saying that the more I have to handle the goods, the higher the chances of getting caught," Jeremy said. "It's all probabilities."

"Probabilities?" boomed Stilton. "Probabilities? I'll give you a probability. Your old man finds out what you're doing and probability is he'll revoke your trust fund."

Stilton forced himself to take a deep breath and go back to the soothing lawyer voice.

"You don't like your dad. I don't like him. So together we make so much dough we don't need him. Look, son, all we have to do is be smart for five years. Then get out."

"Yeah, but I need to keep more distance from the product."

Stilton hated it when Jeremy whined.

"Okay, so use a longer pole. Deliver at night. I don't care what you do. In the meantime, we've got customers who can't get enough of this stuff. Let's keep this money machine cranking here, Sonny Boy. Go now. Go. I got a guy coming in I gotta talk to. You're smart. You're gonna be all right. Now scoot."

Garrett noticed Jeremy's ears were bright red, but he shooed him out the door anyway. Dewey was due any minute. They should not be seen together. He stood and stretched, trying to evaluate how reliable the kid was. He didn't seem to care as much about the money as he did about making trouble for his father. He needed to remember that.

When Clyde knocked on the door, Stilton told him to come in. The haggard old man smelled like mothballs. Stilton gestured for him to put the boxes on the corner of the desk.

"Listen," Dewey said, "this is getting to be a real problem. Cash is piling up so fast that I'm having a hard time figuring out where to stash it. Right now I'm using a busted laundry cart, but sooner or later somebody is going to find it."

"By now, I'd think you could afford a new one," Stilton said.

"That's not the point," said Dewey. "I've never seen so much money in one place."

"So what's the problem with that?"

Stilton couldn't see any problem with it. In fact, it sounded good to him.

"Sooner or later the fire marshal or a cop or somebody is gonna come in, take a look around, and ask me to explain it," Dewey said.

Stilton wondered why everyone he talked to tonight was whining.

"They ain't gonna believe I've been selling soap any more than I do. So just what in the hell is it you've got me selling? Whatever it is, it for damn sure ain't legal."

Garrett let out a big sigh and sat down. He planted his good heel on his desk, reaching forward to grab the cuff of his pants to cross his legs at the ankles. Then he rocked back in his chair, spread his arms wide, and answered.

"All right. You're a smart guy. I knew you would figure it out sooner or later. So I might as well tell you. We ain't selling soap. We're selling dope."

"What?" Dewey stammered.

Stilton hated it when Clyde's mouth opened and closed like he was chewing without putting his teeth in.

"Pot, grass, Mary Jane, weed, whatever you want to call it. The hippies and college kids can't get enough of it, because it's prime stuff."

Stilton watched Clyde turn pale and look for a place to sit. He settled on the arm of a chair because the seat was piled high with papers. Stilton didn't much care. Clyde wiped his eyes with both hands and gave his head a shake.

"What you're telling me is that I am now up to my ass in a drug ring. Am I hearing right?"

"Yep," said Stilton. "You got it. Bar soap is code for Colombian. Liquid stands for Jamaican. Organic means Thailand. It's very simple, really."

"I don't believe it," the old man said.

"Believe it. You're the one who calls it in. They put it on a plane and ship it out the next night. We're not street dealers. We're just the supplier. The dealers on the street take the risk. We take the cash. It's that simple."

Stilton watched Clyde sag. Then he took a deep breath and got angry.

"Jesus Christ, Stilton! First, you get me into blackmail, and then I kill somebody, and now this. My batch of chemicals ain't a flea bite compared to the shit you've dragged me into."

Clyde stood and shook his fist at Stilton.

"I ought to kill you, you lousy son of a bitch!" he ranted.

Stilton shrugged.

"Yeah? Go ahead. That'll help you out a whole lot right now, won't it?"

Dewey fell silent.

"Shit."

Things Dewey just said started registering on Stilton. He pulled his feet down and leaned forward, holding a palm out toward Dewey.

"Hold on a minute. You just blurted out a whole bunch of stuff. Let's go through it one step at a time. What do you mean, blackmail?"

Clyde sank back down on the arm of the chair.

"The picture collection in my bank box. The ones of Senator Randy Bill Stennis playing grab-ass with the ladies. They don't have anything to do with his giving up his seat, do they?"

Stilton touched his fingertips together and thought for a moment before speaking.

"How do you know what was in there?"

"Someone cut the strap on the satchel and sliced open one of the envelopes. The pictures fell out in my lap. What the hell am I supposed to do? I had to put them back in and tape the damned thing shut again."

Dewey braced his hands on his knees and looked at the floor.

"Why didn't you tell me?" Stilton asked.

"What difference would it have made? They went in the box, and I have the only key. Who else would ever need to know?"

Garrett thought about that. He muttered, thinking out loud.

"I'm guessing it was Junior."

He looked up to see Dewey shaking his head. He looked like he was going to cry. Just what he needed. Two damned crybabies in the same night.

"Yeah, well then tell me what he was doing rifling my desk the other night," Dewey said.

"When?"

"The night I killed him."

That made Stilton sit up. He struggled to his feet and came out from behind his desk. He walked over to rest a hand on Clyde's shoulder and use his soothing lawyer voice.

"Hold up now. What do you mean you killed him? This is going way too fast. Back up and tell me exactly what happened."

It took a while. By midnight, several things had become clear. The broom handle business was clearly self-defense. The problem was proving it. However, Clyde's story cleared up something that had been troubling Stilton. He couldn't believe the goons he hired were sick enough to stab a man with a broom handle, pin him under a bulldozer, and watch him die. How many people know how to drive the damn things, anyway? Of course, he kept all that to himself. Still it made him wonder what kind of services he got for two thousand bucks.

Stilton carefully explained things to Clyde Dewey. He was stuck. He had no choice. He was going to have to keep on doing what he was doing for five years. Privately, Stilton wasn't even sure Clyde would live that long.

CHAPTER THIRTY

Setting Up Surveillance

Friday, April 8, 1977

Officer Crocker sat doodling at his desk. He needed to find a way to watch the comings and goings at Blue-Belle Dry Cleaning for several weeks. He picked up the phone and dialed an outfielder from last summer's softball team.

"Hey, Bill, this is Lee Crocker. Something has come up. Can we use the lodge to conduct surveillance downtown?"

Bill managed the local bowling alley. Lee could hear pins falling and folks cheering as clearly as if they were in the next room.

"Let me go into the office for a second."

Crocker swiveled back and forth in his chair, drumming the eraser of a pencil against the telephone. He could actually hear the door closing. It was like turning down the volume on a radio.

"I'm not sure I understood what you're asking me," Bill said. "Try me again."

"We're working a pretty big case," Crocker said. "I can't tell you anything about it, except the lodge hall would give us the room to set up a command post until this thing goes down."

"Like how long are we talking?"

Crocker had no idea.

"Two, maybe three weeks," he said. "No longer than a month, tops. We also want to use the bathroom as a darkroom."

Crocker could hear Bill shuffling paper like he was checking a calendar.

140

"We have a meeting scheduled next week."

"This is kinda important. Can you cancel it?" asked Crocker.

Bill had to think that over.

"Wow. I guess so. We don't have a lot going on right now. But you're gonna have to fill me in on all the details when it's over."

"That's fair. We'll be done before next month's meeting. And, look, Bill, this means a lot to the department. Is there some way we can show our appreciation?"

Crocker was hoping he'd say to forget about it.

"Anybody on the PD who knows how to paint?"

Crocker hated to paint. But he would do it if he had to.

"Not a problem. We know how to paint. You choose the color."

Crocker was getting himself in pretty deep on this one.

"You have no idea how good that sounds. We know it needs to be done, but we couldn't muster enough volunteers."

Crocker could understand why.

"I think we can solve your problem."

"Wow. That'd be great. You can borrow my key. You guys got yourselves a deal."

They chatted awhile. When the call was over, Officer Crocker stared at the phone. He was either going to be a hero or get fired. There was only one way to find out. He went to the chief's office and knocked on the door.

"Come in."

Crocker stepped just inside the door. He was guarding his exit.

"Sir, would it help to set up surveillance across the street from the Blue-Belle Dry Cleaners?"

"You bet."

"Well, I've got the Odd Fellows Lodge for the next month."

"Really," said Jennings. "What's it gonna cost us?"

"It won't even show up on the budget. They buy the paint. We paint our way out the door."

The chief took off his glasses and dropped them on the legal pad in front of him.

"Well done, Lee. How soon can you get set up?"

Crocker let out his breath.

"Is tonight okay?"

"Do it. You're in charge of the detail."

"Yes, sir."

Shortly after midnight, Crocker left the motor pool in the police van. Two squad cars followed him to the curb in front of J. C. Penney's. The vehicles were gone within twenty minutes. By daybreak, Crocker had the cameras in place and the darkroom in operation. He had carried in a large bulletin board and leaned it against the wall. Next to it, on the floor, sat a box of thumb tacks. His crew had set up seven folding tables, each tagged with a day of the week. The operation was underway.

Crocker's team photographed everyone entering and leaving the dry cleaners each day. They spread out the pictures on the tables according to date. Each photo had a date and time written in pencil on the back. By the end of the week, the team began seeing patterns. They could match up customers according to drop-offs and pickups.

Sometimes one spouse would drop off the cleaning and the other would pick it up. The city cops recognized most of them. But the customers who made their own drops and pickups became the focus of their efforts. That's when things got interesting.

Crocker called in Detective Kuhlmann and Sam Whiteside to show them what they found.

"Most folks bring in their stuff and come back a day or two later," he said, "and that's it. They haven't been back. But Clyde has some customers who show up two or three times a week. It kinda stands out, you know what I mean? So far we have identified seven frequent flyers. Roy was the first to see it."

Crocker pointed to one of the guys who raised his hand. Then he led Kuhlmann and Whiteside over to the bulletin board.

"Notice the difference between what they bring in and what they pick up," he said.

Sam and Kuhlmann leaned in close to see. Under the pictures were names the cops had given them: Mustache, Horn Rim, Hook Nose, Chubby, Blackie, and Bow Legs.

"Mustache here brings in a duffle bag full of stuff," Crocker said, "and leaves two days later with two shirt boxes and a pair of slacks."

Kuhlmann got it.

"Look here, Sam," he said. "Here's a guy who brings in a gym bag and later picks up a sport coat."

"I see that," Sam said. "And the next guy brings in a full pillow case and takes home three shirts. My God, it's a regular crime wave. Clyde Dewey is destroying clothing inside there, and his customers are too damn dumb to figure it out. Congratulations, gentlemen."

Crocker knew when he was being messed with.

Kuhlmann caught the twinkle in Sam's eye. He played along.

"Whiteside, you ain't got the sense God gave a goose. What you're looking at is shrinkage, pure and simple."

Having been yanked around enough, Crocker spoke up.

"Or … maybe you geniuses are missing the obvious. They could be hauling in cash from dope sales. Clyde is shoveling something out the back door. Every night he delivers four or five shirt boxes to Tiltin' Stilton's office around seven. That lawyer soiled sixteen shirts this week alone."

"Don't surprise me none," said Kuhlmann. "Everybody in town knows he's dirty."

A number of cops groaned. Kuhlmann decided they had messed with the guys enough.

"Gentlemen," he said, "it looks like you might have found our local dope dealers. Or at least their runners. Figure out who these guys are, and let's dig up everything we can find on them."

"Good work, guys." Sam was serious.

Crocker tried to act nonchalant, but when he looked around the room, everyone was grinning at him. His gamble had just paid off, and it was a great feeling.

CHAPTER THIRTY-ONE

Fish Kill

Thursday, April 14, 1977

Raymond got up early because Tracker needed to go outside. It was still dark. He pulled on a pair of jeans and shoved his bare feet into his shoes. He hesitated in the kitchen long enough to put on the coffee. His untied laces clattered against the linoleum floor when he walked to the door. Tracker bounded through, and Raymond stepped out to enjoy the sweet morning air. But not today. Something stank.

Tracker barked and paced nervously back and forth along the water's edge. Raymond worked his way down to the water, straining to see in the dim light. Hundreds of white objects floated just beneath the surface of the lake. It took him a moment to recognize what he was looking at. Before him were hundreds and hundreds of dead fish.

As the daylight improved, the magnitude of the fish kill became astonishing. He could see that fish weren't the only victims. Turtles, frogs, snakes—everything alive in the water last night now floated belly-up in front of him. Something else hung in the air besides the scent of dead marine life. Something acrid. Man-made. Chemical.

Raymond turned to go back inside to dress. He moved quickly now. Tracker was getting agitated.

"C'mon, boy," he said, dashing for the truck. "Let's get to town and see if we can get Bud out here."

Raymond and Bud were back at the lake three hours later, trying to figure out what had happened. Bud had called the Department of Natural Resources. Dr. Louise Fletcher, a biologist, was still enroute.

144

Raymond sat in the front of the boat, pointing at a cove.

"The biggest concentration seems to be over there," he said.

Bud looked around to see where he pointed and began rowing in that direction.

As they got closer, Raymond could see more features.

"Looks like a creek feeds into it," he said. "Shall we row in there and take a look?"

"Might not hurt," said Bud.

What they saw amazed them. The creek was a trail of death.

The smell made Raymond's stomach churn.

"Looks like we found where it came in," he said.

"I wonder how far upstream we have to go," Bud said. "Do you have any waders?"

"Not here. What do we do now?"

"Let's go back to the cabin and wait for the biologist," Bud said. "She'll need to see this for herself. I'll radio the office and get a deputy to bring out some waders. What do you think? Three pair?"

"That's my guess," Raymond said. "Dr. Fletcher may have her own gear, but it's better to be sure. What we do know is that we need her on this hike."

Raymond looked out over the carcasses in the water and felt a deep sense of sadness. It was hard to imagine what could cause something like this.

When Dr. Fletcher arrived, she introduced herself. She was just a little over five feet tall, a girl from Arkansas who fell in love with fishing as a kid. She had a Southern twang in her voice, but it didn't take long to see that she was bright. Bud and Raymond filled her in. She listened and asked a few pointed questions, some they could answer, some they could not. Then they told her about the creek.

"Let's go," she said. "No telling how far upstream we will have to go to find the spill site."

"Spill site?" Raymond asked. "How do you know there is a spill site?"

"You don't think this is an act of God, do you?" she said. "I've seen it too many times. Somebody's dumped toxic chemicals in here, and we need to find out where and what it was. Hiking up the creek is about as good a way as any."

They applied mosquito repellant and got back in the boat. Dr. Fletcher started making field notes about what sort of fish and animals were dead, and how many she counted.

"Counting dead critters is just about the simplest way there is to show the magnitude of the spill," she explained.

They took her to the mouth of the creek and tied the boat to a tree. As they started climbing out, Bud got a call from dispatch on his handheld radio. Lucy passed on an update from Sam about the surveillance on the dry cleaners.

Raymond was listening intently to Dr. Fletcher's running narrative as they sloshed upstream. She was pointing out how even the vegetation along the creek bank was beginning to die.

That waterway, once lush and beautiful, was now a trail of death and destruction. Three and a half miles upstream, they found the crime scene at a boat ramp beneath the Highway HH Bridge.

"The chemicals are going to contaminate this whole fishing and swimming area for a year or more," Dr. Fletcher said. "We're gonna have to post signs to keep people out of here."

Bud showed Raymond the fresh tire tracks in the mud. The smell of turpentine, coal oil, and other solvents stung their noses and made their eyes water.

"How will this affect the public water system?" Raymond asked.

"Hard to say," came her answer. "It all depends on what chemicals we find in the samples. Once we identify them, we can figure out how to treat it. The folks at the municipal water treatment plant are waiting on these samples. So I better get them to the lab."

Raymond's nose told him a great deal. He was wading in water polluted with solvents. He recognized acetone, MEK, and gasoline. On the dirt trail down to the boat launch, Bud made an important find.

"Look at this, Ray," he said.

He picked up a lid from a Ball canning jar that had been mashed down into the mud. It had a ragged three-inch piece of masking tape on it, apparently used for a label. The writing was still legible. Someone had written 'Stoddard' on it with a marker.

"Do you know anyone by that name?" Raymond asked

"No. Can't say I do," Bud said thoughtfully.

"Let me see that a moment," asked Dr. Fletcher.

She studied the lid for a moment before she handed it back to the sheriff.

"If you're thinking it's somebody's name, you may not have much luck. Some years back, dry cleaners used an agent called Stoddard solvent. From what we've seen today, that would be my first guess. The lab work will tell us for sure."

Bud held up the jar lid to Raymond.

"Let's keep this part out of the paper. It's key evidence. Only the real perp would know about it."

"Gotcha," Raymond said. "You know, between the dead fish and chemicals, I don't think I'm gonna eat for days."

CHAPTER THIRTY-TWO

Unraveling

Tuesday, April 19, 1977

Raleigh Journal-Messenger

By Raymond Thornton, Contributing Editor

During the night of April 14, 1977, a person or persons unknown murdered thousands of helpless residents of Raleigh County in their sleep. The unidentified culprit killed every living creature in Lake Osage with one heedless act. I know. I discovered it.

By noon, Sheriff Bud Oswald, Dr. Louise Fletcher, a biologist with the Missouri Department of Natural Resources, and I hiked up to the source on Miller Creek.

Dr. Fletcher says that it may take years to undo the damage and restore the habitat. She will turn her findings over to the U.S. Environmental Protection Agency for further investigation and prosecution.

On a personal note, never have I seen a more contemptible act in an agricultural county whose very soil and water are our lifeblood.

The decisions Andy Russell made at Indianapolis that night were fateful ones. He would be on instruments throughout the flight due to widespread low clouds and fog. The freezing level was around four thousand feet, so he intended to climb above it and cruise in the clear at six thousand. It was a nice plan, and it might have worked if there hadn't been an occluded front in the way.

Negotiating imbedded thunderstorms without weather radar was like playing Russian roulette. He had an instrument ticket, but he really didn't understand weather. Tonight would remedy that.

He bought enough fuel to give himself three-and-a-half hours of flight time before packing the payload in the Cessna's back seat and luggage bay. He wanted to stay under his maximum weight limits. It was a novice pilot's mistake. A veteran would never leave extra fuel on the ground in weather like this.

He gave himself three hours to reach Raleigh with a half-hour reserve. Meanwhile, he filed an instrument flight plan full of lies. He listed four-and-a-half hours of fuel on board and identified Claremont as his alternate. One thing was certain: he wasn't about to land anywhere else with three hundred fifty pounds of dope in his plane, so it didn't really matter. Raleigh was his only destination.

The first surprise that night was that a loaded Cessna with ice on its wings could barely stagger to six thousand feet. The problem wasn't only on the wings. Ice in the carburetor threatened to strangle the engine's fuel supply. He had to pull on full carburetor heat, which made the engine run rich. Then he had to lean the mixture and shove in full throttle to maintain adequate power. Consequently, he had no idea how fast he was burning fuel. Sweat trickled down his back for two hours while air traffic control steered him around thunderstorms.

It was a rough flight. Flashes of lightning blinded him, so he turned the cockpit lights to full brightness. Fatigue was eating him alive. His instrument scan broke down. He caught himself fixating on one instrument at a time, followed by exaggerated corrections. He ate a bar of chocolate for an energy boost.

After an exhausting two-and-a-half hours, Air Traffic Control cleared him from six to four thousand feet. It was the start of his descent into Raleigh. He began picking up ice at four thousand feet. He knew he couldn't stay there long, so he asked for lower. The controller cleared him down to three.

"Kansas City Center, Cessna five zero eight three two."

"Cessna eight three two. Center, go ahead."

"Cessna eight three two, thanks for your help tonight. I've just broken out in the clear, and I can see the ground. I'll cancel my instrument flight plan at this time."

"Roger, understand you are cancelling instrument flight rules. Squawk twelve hundred and have a good flight."

"Cessna eight three two, squawking twelve hundred. Good night."

It was his final lie. He was still in the clouds, droning along in uncontrolled airspace without a clearance. At this hour, he was betting on the 'big sky, little airplane' theory to avoid a midair collision.

He reviewed the instrument approach chart, set up his inbound course on the number one navigation radio, and dialed up the first step-down fix on number two. He eased his way down to twenty-six hundred feet and crossed the initial approach fix inbound, waiting, waiting, waiting for the side-bearing needle to center. It oscillated slightly and slowly began to center.

Close enough for me, he thought. *Now down to fifteen hundred feet, level off, and wait for the airport.*

The approach would position him over the middle of the field without lining him up with any runway. He would have to pick one and circle to land. To be successful, he had to perform two conflicting tasks: keep his eyes on the airport while also keeping them on the altimeter. It was the worst of all possible instrument approaches.

While waiting for the needles to tell him he was over the airport, he realized his cockpit lights were still at full intensity. Hastily, he cranked them down. His night vision was all screwed up. The needles centered. He was there. And he was completely blind to the surface lighting. It was time to go around.

What the hell is my missed approach procedure?

He shoved in the power, stabilized his climb straight ahead, and glanced down at the approach chart to find the missed approach procedure. It was hard to see in the dim lights.

Climbing left turn to twenty-six hundred feet, fly outbound on the approach course, and hold at the intersection northeast. His eyes went back to the instruments to discover he was in a six-hundred-feet-per-minute descending left turn. Rapidly he leveled the wings and reestablished the climb. He began chanting the missed approach procedure out loud.

"Climbing left turn to twenty-six hundred, back to the intersection, hold northeast, climbing left turn to twenty-six hundred, back to the intersection, hold northeast …"

With sweat dripping into his eyes, he struggled to keep his wits about him. He backtracked along the inbound course to the intersection and made a sloppy turn into the holding pattern. Things finally settled down so he could think.

The cockpit lights are dim now. My eyes have had time to adjust. I'll have to shoot the approach all over again. Goddammit! I forgot to activate the runway lights. No wonder I couldn't see shit.

He exhaled forcefully before drawing in a big breath of air and prepared himself to slog through the entire approach again. He set the communication radio to 122.7 in order to activate the lights. *Okay. Here we go. Out for the procedure turn, and then do it all over again.*

He abandoned the holding pattern and tracked away from the airport for one full minute. Then he made a forty-five-degree right turn, rolled wings level, and checked the clock. A minute later, he started a shallow left turn and headed back to intercept the inbound course. Time slowed to a crawl. That decision cost him six minutes of fuel. He refused to glance at the gauges. The last thing he needed now was another distraction.

He joined the inbound course and waited for his step-down fix. A minute and a half later, he crossed it and began his descent to fifteen hundred feet.

Keep the needle centered. Approaching minimums, ease in the throttle to stop the descent, wings level. Steady. Steady. Wait for the missed approach point.

He keyed the mike five times to bring up the approach lights. *There! I see something glowing!*

While looking outside, his altitude sagged below minimums. He was only four hundred feet above ground instead of seven hundred. He didn't know, because his eyes were trying to make sense out of the runway lights. He decided to land on runway 24, crossed midfield, and began a left-hand pattern to keep the runway in sight. That's when the engine quit. The silence was tranquil … and horrifying.

Back on the gauges, he discovered he was three hundred feet above ground in a forty-degree bank, sinking five hundred feet per minute. He rolled the wings level, slowed to best glide, and hung out full flaps to minimize the speed of impact. Staring straight ahead into the blackness, he had only one idea left. He turned on the landing light and uttered his last words.

"Oh shit."

CHAPTER THIRTY-THREE

Airport Surveillance

Wednesday, April 20, 1977

Cassius Greene drew a rookie named Tim for night watch at the airport. He didn't know the guy very well. Tonight would fix that. The weather was so crappy Cassius knew it would be a long, boring night. To stay awake, he asked Tim about cars, women, the best restaurants he'd ever been in, his favorite movies, and food.

"How come you wanted to be a deputy?" Cassius asked. "Can't you find a real job?"

"Raleigh County has been good to me. I just want to pay something back," Tim replied.

"Humph," said Cassius.

He'd heard that one before. It was Tim's public answer, not his private one. He watched the fog drift across the field. Water droplets collected on the windshield of the cruiser. He turned to say something about it when Tim started twisting his head around.

"Do you hear something?" Tim asked.

It was as quiet as a graveyard out here. He didn't need a spooked rookie.

"What the hell are you talking about? I don't hear nothin' …"

"Shhh, listen! Crank down your window," said Tim.

He was right. The sound of an airplane engine grew distinct, and then it passed.

"You gotta be shittin' me," Cassius said. "What kind of damn fool would be out flying on a night like this?"

He and Tim looked at each other for a moment.

"You thinking what I'm thinking?" Tim asked.

"Aw, come on, man. Not even a dope runner could be that stupid," Cassius said.

It started to rain.

"That's exactly what I'm thinking," said Tim.

"I don't even like to drive on a night like this, let alone go fly in some little popknocker. But maybe we better call in and get the cops on the kid with the Mustang."

Tim made the radio call. Dispatch said they would relay the message. They sat in the cool, clammy night air, windows down and heater running, listening for an airplane and watching fog drift around the airport.

"I don't suppose he'll come back, will he?" Tim asked.

Cassius was having a premonition. The hair prickled on the back of his neck.

"I don't know what to think."

They sat in silence for fifteen minutes. Suddenly the runway lights came on and they both jumped.

"Hang on here, partner. This could get interesting."

Then they heard it again, this time lower and closer.

"I saw red and green lights," Cassius said.

He stepped out of the car to watch and listen.

Tim got out on his side.

"I did, too."

Suddenly the engine sound quit. It sputtered once and went silent. They stared across the roof of the cruiser at each other, wide-eyed. Cassius began counting potatoes.

"One potato, two potatoes, three potatoes, four potatoes …"

He was up to thirty-three when they heard a distant sound of cracking timber followed by a thump. Then everything was still.

In disbelief, Cassius looked at Tim. His partner was turning pale.

"If you are gonna throw up," Cassius said, "this'd be a good time to get it over with, because I think we're gonna be busy."

Cassius watched Tim thinking about it. Then the rookie placed a hand on the door, doubled over, and did it. When he was done, he stood up, wiping his face with a handkerchief. They got back in the car and pulled the doors shut.

"How in the hell are we gonna find him in this fog?" Cassius said, looking over at Tim.

"I dunno. Maybe look for a fire?"

"Better call it in."

Cassius was planning to get everybody out prowling the back roads around the airport, using their spotlights to find something all torn up.

That's when a car pulled into the airport parking lot.

"Who is that?" asked Tim.

"I don't know. It's a Mustang, Shelby Cobra. Must be the Bryce kid."

"What do we do?"

"I say we read him his rights," Cassius said.

He gunned the engine and sped around the corner of the hangar. He raced across the parking lot to skid to a stop behind the green Mustang. Cassius opened his door and then stepped outside the cruiser. He searched with his flashlight until he found the driver's face. It was Jeremy Bryce.

Cassius transferred his flashlight to his left hand, keeping it in Jeremy's face. He stepped away from the cruiser and pulled his service revolver, holding it low in his right hand. Cassius clicked off the safety.

Out of the corner of his eye, he saw Tim drop to one knee and aim his gun with both hands through the back window. Cassius spoke casually and with a reassuring tone.

"Good evening, Mr. Bryce. How's it going? Sir, I'm gonna ask you to step out of the car, but please do it slowly. Keep both hands in plain sight. Thank you. We'd like to ask you a few questions, if you don't mind."

CHAPTER THIRTY-FOUR

Blackberries

Thursday, April 21, 1977

Bud was tired and frustrated. Searching the back roads all night had been fruitless. He asked the airport manager for an aerial search at first daylight, but it took until eight thirty before the call came in.

"Bud, the pilot found what looks like a wreck half a mile northeast of Creekside Lane and County Road NN, in a stand of timber."

"Okay, ask Sam meet me at that intersection, and we'll hike in to take a look," Bud said.

When Sam arrived, Bud was standing by the road trying to figure out the most efficient way to get to the site. "About a half mile northeast" started to sound pretty vague when you had to choose which barbed wire fences to climb over. Bud needed the pilot to talk them in there. He asked Lucy to work it out.

"Okay, Sam," Bud said. "Here's the deal. We have four objectives for this little field trip: find the wreck, look for survivors, get the tail number, and see if there is any pot on board."

"That's it?" asked Sam.

"No. That's it for this trip. Everything else will have to wait until we get instructions from the FAA and NTSB."

"Oh, I get it. Like the first look at a crime scene. Disturb as little evidence as possible."

"That's my thinking. But we're in for a long day," Bud said.

"Gotcha."

Dispatch called on Bud's radio.

"Sheriff, the pilot doesn't have a way to talk to you directly," Lucy told him, "but we have worked out a relay. He can talk to the airport manager by radio. I will patch him into to your portable. Will that work?"

"It will have to do. Let me know when everyone's ready."

"The pilot says he will fly over your location to give you a line to start with. Then he will orbit and talk you in."

Without guidance from the circling aircraft, they would have missed it. The undergrowth in the timber was dense. Suddenly, they stepped out into a clearing in the woods that did not exist yesterday. It took a while for Bud's mind to start registering what he was seeing. It wasn't trash; it was debris.

Sam pointed to a large piece of white sheet metal wrapped around a tree about twenty feet up.

"Wing?" he asked.

"Could be. Where's the other one?"

They found it on the ground lying in the middle of a stand of blackberries.

"Okay, Sam. Look up," Bud said. "You can see where he cut a swath through those top branches."

Bud turned to look at blue sky through the notch in the timber.

"So if he entered here," he said, pointing with his left hand, "he must be over there."

He pointed in the opposite direction with his right.

"Look up in that big oak," said Sam, "about twelve feet up. Limbs broken and all the bark skinned off. There's the tail upside-down over there."

"Then that pile of rubbish on the ground may be the cockpit," said Bud.

"Oh shit," said Sam.

"Oh shit indeed."

Bud removed his hat and ran his fingers through his hair. He tugged his hat back on and stood for a while with his fists on his hips.

"Okay," he said. "No point in both of us trampling around in there. You stay here, and I'll go."

Bud got the tail number: N50832. He saw twisted human remains and turned away. He didn't want to puke in front of Sam. Bags of marijuana were everywhere—some torn open, some still intact. He picked one up off the ground and carried it over to Sam.

"Here you go," he said. "Let's get out of here and call the Feds."

"We're gonna be covered with ticks tonight. I hate 'em," said Sam.

"Me too," said Bud.

Lucy patched him into the Flight Service Station in Claremont. A flight school in the Bootheel reported an overdue aircraft. The Flight Service Station relayed Bud's report to Flight Standards in St. Louis, along with his question: "What happens next?" By ten o'clock, an FAA inspector called Bud through dispatch. The battery on his portable unit was dead, so he was using his truck radio.

"Sheriff, this is Inspector Darryl Cooke. Where are you right now?"

"I'm standing on a gravel road not far from the crash site," Bud said.

"Did you see a tail number?" asked Cooke.

"Yes. It was November five zero eight three two."

"Any survivors?" the inspector asked.

"Not from what I saw. I know we've got at least one very dead guy. So what do I do next?" Bud asked.

"Handle it like a homicide," said Cooke. "How many people have been to the site?"

"Two. Just a deputy and me."

"Okay, Sheriff. Here's what we'll do," said Cooke. "Have the medical examiner go in and remove any victims. Photograph the position of the bodies first. No one else goes in until I get there. Say an hour and a half, maybe two hours. How do I find you?"

"I can meet you at the airport office. I'll lead you in from there."

"Easy enough," said Cooke. "Technically, this crash belongs to the NTSB. I'm going to call them before I head out. They will do one of two things. One of their guys will fly in from Chicago, or they'll delegate it to me. I'll know by the time I get there."

"Okay, but there's something else you need to know," said Bud.

"What's that?"

"This guy got hammered between a tree and a truckload of marijuana. We busted a drug ring this morning on account of him. We need evidence to make our case," Bud told him.

"No problem," said Cooke. "We all work together and everybody gets what they need."

"Sounds good. What did you say your name was?"

"Daryl Cooke, C-o-o-k-e."

"Didn't I talk to you a while back?" Bud asked.

"Seems like."

"This is the same plane I called you about."

"I remember now. Don't that beat all?"

CHAPTER THIRTY-FIVE

The Logbook

Thursday, April 21, 1977

Sheriff Bud Oswald entered the interrogation room about six thirty that night. With him was Deputy Cassius Greene. Bud bumped the table to wake Jeremy Bryce up from a nap, and sat down to join him. Deputy Greene leaned against the wall. Bud put a cold Coke in front of Jeremy without a word. The kid looked at him suspiciously.

"It's okay," Bud said. "That's for you. I know it's been a long day."

Jeremy pulled the tab off the can and took a big gulp.

"I understand you have been asking for your lawyer all day," Bud said.

Jeremy shrugged and took another swig of Coke.

"No lawyer, no questions. You know how it is," he said.

Bud crossed his legs at the knee and seemed relaxed.

"I understand that. I just came by to introduce myself. You probably remember Deputy Greene. He's the one who arrested you. He tells me you have quite a car. Mustang, is it?"

Bud watched Jeremy debate whether or not to respond.

"Yeah," Jeremy said.

Bud gestured at Deputy Greene.

"He says he's not sure one of our cruisers could keep up with you. What do you think?"

"About what?" Jeremy asked.

Bud watched his eyes. Jeremy was trying to act indifferent.

"If we had an old-fashioned car chase," Bud said, "you think a little old Mustang could outrun a police car?"

Jeremy pointed at Bud and squinted.

"Well, see, that's the thing. It isn't just a little old Mustang. It's a Shelby."

Bud uncrossed his legs and leaned forward, bracing his elbows on his knees. He acted keenly interested in Jeremy's car.

"You mean, like in a Cobra 500?"

"Yeah."

Bud sat back and thought about it.

"Whew! That's quite a car," he said. "What kind of motor do they put in those things, anyhow?"

"Mine is a GT 500. It has a 428 in it," Jeremy answered.

Bud seemed truly impressed.

"You mean, like in cubic inches?" he asked.

"Yeah. That's what I mean."

Bud sat back and shook his head in amazement.

"Wow. That's something," he said. "It's got a distinctive sort of look to it, too, doesn't it?"

"Yeah. People notice."

Bud turned to look at Deputy Greene.

"Do we see many of those around here, Cassius?"

"Naw. Can't say there are a lot of them around," said the deputy.

Bud asked Deputy Greene another question.

"Except for last night, when would you say was the last time we noticed one of those around here?"

"Well, let's see," the deputy said.

He started digging through a file folder.

"Here's a picture of one we took a few nights ago," he said, "out at the airport. It's parked with its trunk open next to this airplane."

Deputy Greene placed a photograph on the table.

"Even though this picture is infrared," the deputy said, "you can't miss the Mustang lines and that little thingy on the hood. Hmm. Look at this, Sheriff."

The deputy turned the picture toward Bud and pointed at a figure.

"This guy right here hauling an armload of stuff resembles Mr. Bryce, wouldn't you say?"

Bud went with it. He looked at the picture and then at Jeremy several times.

"It sure does," he said. "When exactly was that taken, Cassius?"

The deputy turned it over and read the label on the back.

"Says here it was taken April 16 at 3:23 AM."

Bud turned to look at Jeremy.

"That's kinda interesting, wouldn't you say, Jeremy?"

The kid didn't answer. Bud understood why. He looked at Deputy Greene again.

"Have we ever seen anything like this before?" he asked.

"Well, let's see," the deputy said. "I've got pictures of three other occasions like this one here. All the cars look the same, and even the airplane and the people. Same license plate and everything."

"What dates, Cassius?" asked the sheriff.

"April 8, April 11, and April 13, seems like."

"Anything else?" Bud asked.

"Yeah," Deputy Greene said. "These shots here. They were taken in broad daylight on March 25. They show Mr. Bryce fishing out that two-kilo bag of pot we planted in the dumpster behind the Gamma House. We got a close-up of his face, and a real good one of his license plate."

Bud slowly reached behind his back and pulled something out of his belt. Jeremy flinched.

"Now, no need to get all jittery on me," Bud said. "I just wanted to ask you if you have ever seen one of these."

He held up a thin black book with the words "Flight Log" embossed on the front. It was badly creased and covered with smudges.

Jeremy was silent.

"You ever see one of these things before?" Bud asked again.

"Naw," Jeremy said.

"Well, this one is sorta interesting. We pulled it out of an airplane wreck this afternoon. It used to belong to a guy named Andy Russell. Do you know anyone by that name?" Bud asked.

"I don't think so."

"Take your time. You want to be sure about this now."

Bud noticed Jeremy was getting fidgety. Good.

"Look, I already told you, I don't know him."

"That's mighty interesting, see," Bud said, "because old Andy seemed to be very conscientious about logging his flight time. Let's see what's in here."

Bud opened the book and thumbed through it to the most recent entries.

"We got a whole lot of flights from Indianapolis to Raleigh in here. One on April 8, another on April 11, one for April 13, and the most recent on the sixteenth. There's even one here dated March 24. These dates kind of match up, wouldn't you say, between this logbook and our pictures? And look here," Bud said, opening the back cover. "It even has your name and phone number written in it. Looks like Andy's handwriting even."

"I want my lawyer."

"Of course you do. And just who in particular would that be?" Bud asked

"Garrett Stilton."

"Well, see now. That's a problem."

Bud crossed his legs again and placed his hands in his lap.

"We've been trying to reach him for you all day, but he doesn't answer his phone," Bud said. "We even sent some people out to look for him. No luck. You don't suppose he skipped town and left you holding the bag, do you, Jeremy? Does that seem possible to you?"

"Then I need a different lawyer."

Bud pointed his index finger skyward.

"Now, see, I believe that is an excellent idea," he said. "We'll get right on that. Meantime, you think about our little chat here. If you start remembering stuff that can help us do our job, it might work to your advantage, you know what I mean?"

Bud stood. Then he motioned for Cassius to come with him. They left the kid sitting all alone, one hand shackled to the table leg, the other sliding a can of Coke around in a small wet circle on the table top.

CHAPTER THIRTY-SIX

Who Is Stoddard?

Thursday, April 21, 1977

Clyde Dewey scurried down Main Street with five shirt boxes under his chin. He felt conspicuous. He heard about the plane crash this morning. He had never been more terrified in his life. He used to think of himself as an honorable man, but now he couldn't keep score. Let's see. He had killed a man. He had killed thousands of fish. He had poisoned Raleigh's drinking water, and now he was walking down Main Street with an armload of drug money, acting like an honest man. How could people not see him for what he was—human filth? There was no solvent strong enough to cleanse his wretched soul.

He scanned the street for anything suspicious. He didn't see anything out of order. That made him even more nervous. Passing the drug store, he turned into the doorway leading to Tiltin' Stilton's law office and charged up the stairs, watching his feet to avoid missing a step. When he hit the landing, he found himself looking at two men. They were leaning against the wall on either side of Stilton's door. One of them spoke to him by name.

"Good evening, Clyde. I'm Detective Kuhlmann, Raleigh police. Perhaps you know Deputy Whiteside here?"

"Uh, I don't think we've met. Uh, I mean I know who he is and all."

Clyde saw the deputy flash him a big smile and reach out to shake hands. Instinctively, he shifted the boxes to his left arm and held out his right hand. The deputy grabbed his hand and pumped it so vigorously

Clyde fumbled all five boxes. Bundles of bills spilled out when they hit the floor.

"My goodness, Mr. Dewey," the detective said. "Who would have thought the dry cleaning business was so lucrative? Sam, looks like you and me got into the wrong line of work."

"Guess so," the deputy said.

"So, Clyde," the detective continued, "tell us, what's your secret to success?"

"Well, uh ..."

Clyde knelt down and hastily tried to cram the money back inside the boxes.

"Here, here!" the detective said. "Let us help you with that."

Both men bent down to help scoop the money back into the boxes. When the deputy stood up, he tucked a box under one arm. The detective collected a couple more.

Now Clyde held only two boxes of money. Detective Kuhlmann put an arm around his shoulder and gently steered him back down the stairs.

"What say the three of us go back to your place and have a little talk," the detective said. "I haven't been in a dry cleaning shop in a while. Maybe you can give us a little tour, kinda show us what goes on back there."

Dewey noticed that the deputy stayed between him and the street, while the detective on the other side kept an arm around him like they were long-lost war buddies. Clyde couldn't think. Kuhlmann kept talking about the weather, the Cardinals, and anything that popped into his head. He bombarded Clyde with questions that came faster than he could answer.

Before he knew it, he found himself corralled between two big guys in front of his shop. Accepting his fate, he fished out his key and unlocked the door.

The detective and the deputy dumped their boxes of money on the counter like there was nothing in them but shirts. Then they steered him back into his office. Dewey sank down in his chair, a defeated man.

"Nice place you got here," Kuhlmann said, looking around.

He sat on the corner of Dewey's desk, making Clyde look up at him. He leaned in close.

"Sam here is doing a little research," said the detective. "You might be able to help him."

"Sure. I mean … if I can help," Dewey said.

He wrung his hands and turned to the deputy, trying to figure out what was coming next.

"Well, see," the deputy began, "we are trying to find somebody named Stoddard. Do you know anyone by that name?"

Clyde shook his head. He looked perplexed.

"No. I can't say that I do."

"See," the deputy continued, "Sheriff Oswald found something with that name on it. He wants to find the rightful owner. It says Stoddard on it."

Clyde wondered just what in the hell he was up to. The deputy suddenly snapped his fingers.

"I don't know what I was thinking," he said. "I have it right here in my pocket."

He fished out the canning jar lid and handed it to Clyde.

Clyde's mouth fell open. He was speechless. How?

"See?" said the deputy, pointing. "Somebody wrote his name on it right there. You ever see anything like this before?"

Clyde slowly shook his head, mouth agape.

"Okay, so let me tell you how he found it," the deputy continued. "Did you hear about the big fish kill in Lake Osage?"

"Yeah, I read about it in the paper," Clyde said.

He wasn't a good liar, and he knew it. The deputy kept squeezing him.

"Well, the sheriff waded up Miller Creek with this lady biologist from the state until they found a place where a bunch of chemicals had been dumped. They just kept going until they ran out of dead fish.

That's where they found this. In the mud on the boat ramp. You ever seen anything like this?"

"No, I've never seen that before in my life."

Clyde was lying. They both knew he was lying. He knew they knew. And they knew he knew they knew. That's when the deputy went in for the kill.

"Well, let me change the question slightly. Instead of asking *who* Stoddard is, what if I asked you *what* Stoddard is? Does that do anything for you?"

Clyde fell into the trap, but he couldn't help it. He couldn't think of a way out.

"Oh, well, now," he said, being way too helpful, "in the old days, dry cleaners used Stoddard solvent. But that's about all I can think of."

The deputy looked at him silently. He took the lid out of Clyde's hand and fanned it in the air. Then the deputy looked at the detective.

"Now see, Bob, that's what I was telling you. That biologist said the water was chock full of all kinds of solvents. So where do you suppose something like that could come from?"

"It's a mystery to me," said the detective with a shrug.

Clyde knew he was done for. These guys weren't gonna let up.

"You know, Clyde," said the deputy, "we're working on another mystery. Maybe you can help us out with this one, too. We found Junior Petiole dead at the city dump, mounted on a broom handle, kinda like the one you bought the next day at Ace Hardware. How do you figure something like that could happen?"

Clyde sagged like a wet towel. He tried to think for a moment, his mouth opening and closing, but no words came out.

"Okay. All right," Clyde said. "You're gonna find out anyhow. That was self-defense. He started to pull a gun on me. I had to do it to save myself. It was the only way I could stop him."

"By turning him into a corn dog?"

"It was horrible. This big gun was coming at my face. I jammed it in as hard as I could. He dropped the gun and grabbed the stick with both hands, but he couldn't pull it out.

"Wow, that had to be awful," the deputy said.

"You know," said Kuhlmann, "this is important, you telling us all this. But it sounds like a long story. What say we go get your broom, collect those boxes of money out front, and head over to the police station where we can sort all this out."

Clyde held out his hands, wrists together for cuffs. His eyes watered and he swallowed a sob.

"Hey, I know this is not easy," said the detective. "But we don't need to put cuffs on you or anything, do we?"

Clyde shook his head no and wiped his runny nose with his hand. Kuhlmann leaned over to place a gentle hand on his shoulder.

"Look," he said, "we pretty much know how you got sucked into this mess. We are really after Stilton. Will you help us?"

Clyde nodded his head and stood up slowly. Without a word, he stepped into the store room and came out carrying an old broom with a new handle. The detective gently placed an arm around the old man's shoulder.

"Let's get your money and give you a chance to tell us how all this happened," he said.

Clyde took a ragged breath and sighed. He was glad it was over.

CHAPTER THIRTY-SEVEN

Preliminary Accident Report

Friday, April 29, 1977

Sheriff Bud Oswald returned from the courthouse to find a stack of phone messages waiting for him. The most interesting one was from Inspector Darryl Cooke, the FAA guy. The message said, "He has some new information for you."

Bud returned that call first.

"Thanks for all your help," Cooke said. "Your pictures are part of our accident report. I listened to the ATC tapes and got a radar track for the flight leading up to the crash. I need to go to Claremont Monday afternoon. Can we meet for lunch? What's the name of that place in town?"

"You talking about Dutch's?" Bud asked.

He had enjoyed working with Cooke. The man was methodical about forensic evidence and wouldn't begin to speculate until he had all the facts. He had given Andy Russell's logbook to Bud. All he wanted was a copy, so he used the department's copy machine.

"Yeah, that's the one. Will eleven work for you?"

"I will make it work," Bud said. "So what's the new information?"

"Would you believe me if I told you Andy Russell was a liar?" Cooke asked.

"Why, inspector, I am shocked," Bud said. "A nice young drug runner like that?"

"Hard to believe, isn't it? He lied on his flight plan, and he lied to air traffic control. I thought you might find transcripts of the tape and a copy of his radar track helpful. I can go over them with you on Monday."

"Okay if I bring Deputy Whiteside with me?" Bud asked. "He's the one heading up our investigation."

"Sure. In fact, tell him I said hello. See you guys on Monday then?" Cooke asked.

"See you then."

Bud called Dutch to get the booth in back. It was the most private. He and Sam got there a few minutes early and were having coffee when Darryl Cooke arrived. The man was all business. Bud liked that. After saying hello, he handed Sam a manila envelope labeled "ATC Transcript, N50832, Raleigh Municipal Airport, April 20–21, 1977."

"You will find this interesting reading. The pilot told ATC he was out of the clouds so he canceled his instrument flight plan. If that were true, the radar track would show him flying directly to the airport and landing," Cooke said.

"I take it that is not what he did," said Sam.

"No, it's not."

Bud signaled Dutch to bring coffee over for Inspector Cooke. Dutch took their orders and wandered back to the kitchen.

"Here, let me show you," Cooke said.

He pulled two sheets of paper out of the envelope.

"Here's his radar track," he said. "And this one is an instrument approach for the airport."

He turned them around to face Bud and Sam so they could study them side by side as Cooke used his pen as a pointer.

"Instead of going right to the airport, he flies the transition route to the instrument approach. Then he shoots the approach and gets below radar. Suddenly, he pops back up and flies the missed approach procedure back here to hold in this little race track."

"So what does that mean?" Bud asked.

"When a pilot shoots an instrument approach and can't see the runway, he makes a missed approach," Cooke explained. "Then he goes to a holding fix until he can decide what to do next, shoot the approach again or divert to an alternate airport."

"Break it down for me," said Sam. "Make it simple."

"Russell claims he is in the clear, but he shoots an instrument approach without talking to air traffic. That is a no-no. He misses the approach and goes back to hold, still not talking to ATC. Another no-no. Then he does something really stupid that gets him killed," Cooke said.

He makes eye contact, first with Sam and then with Bud.

"Here's what killed him," Cooke said.

Cooke pointed his pen at the race-track-shaped holding pattern on the approach chart.

"Holding patterns are set up to line you up for another approach. You are already heading toward the airport," Cooke said. "But look at his radar track. He abandons a perfectly good holding pattern, flies away from the airport, goes out to do a standard procedure turn, and burns six to eight minutes of fuel."

"Wait a minute," said Sam, now holding up both pieces of paper. "You're saying if he had only shot the approach out of the holding pattern …"

"He would have arrived over the airport with six minutes of fuel left in the tanks," said Cooke, "enough to get him on the runway before the engine quit."

Bud watched Cooke sit back and grin. Sam shook both papers.

"Why cut the fuel so close?" he asked.

"He lied," Cooke said. "Guy claims on his flight plan he has four and a half hours of fuel, but he flames out three and a half hours after takeoff."

Bud shook his head. Something about that seemed off.

"Why would you do something that stupid?" he asked.

When Bud looked over at inspector Cooke he realized the man was almost beside himself with glee.

"So you can cram as much pot inside the airplane as possible," he said.

Cooke's eyes twinkled.

"Of course," Bud said, finally taking it all in.

Cooke pointed at the radar track again, this time at the procedure turn.

"Right here," he said, "is where Andy Russell decided to die. Everything after that was just running out the clock."

Bud studied the diagram for a moment. Then he made eye contact with Cooke.

"Darryl," said Bud, "it is a genuine pleasure to meet someone else who lives to break the code."

Cooke took a sip of coffee, eyes dancing.

"It's kinda hard to explain to ordinary folks, ain't it?" he said. "The buzz of putting the puzzle together?"

Bud sat back and smiled.

"Yeah, it really is," he said.

Dutch showed up with a tray full of food. As they ate, their conversation was animated and punctuated with laughter. Bud understood they weren't celebrating Andy Russell's death. They were celebrating solving the riddle behind it.

CHAPTER THIRTY-EIGHT

Bryce Wants Stilton

Monday, May 2, 1977

Walter Bryce stood motionless at the floor-to-ceiling window in his office, looking out over Lambert St. Louis International Airport. He shoved his hands into his pockets while he considered the phone call he had just finished. Stilton had dragged Jeremy into some deep shit. Walter sighed, wiped his forehead with one hand, and turned to sit down in his chair. He placed a fingertip on the intercom button and summoned his secretary.

As she slipped into the room, he gestured for her to have a seat. She sat down and produced her steno pad and pen. He motioned for her to put it away. He stood up and looked out the window again, lost in thought. He glanced over at her and then returned his gaze to the airport. While Walter spoke, his back to her, airplanes took off and landed.

"Do you remember the conversation we had with Stilton the day hell froze over?" Walter asked.

He gave her time to remember. She had an uncanny ability to sense where his thoughts were going. He wondered if this time she might miss. She pondered his question.

"I do," she answered. "That call from Jeremy ... was it bad news?"

Walter looked at her in surprise. He was amazed at how well she could read him.

"Not the best I've ever had," he said. "He's in jail. Stilton conned him into an illegal enterprise. When the cops caught on, Stilton hit the road and left Jeremy holding the bag."

Walter drove his fists into his pockets again. He wanted to grab things and throw them and smash them. But that was not his professional persona. So he used his pockets. When he glanced over his shoulder, she was studying him, her head slightly cocked.

"Oh goodness," she said. "That really is bad news. It raises some other complications, too, doesn't it?"

Walter frequently left her questions unanswered. But this time he turned to face her. He slouched and felt old. Very old. He stared at the Oriental rug in the middle of his office and spoke almost absent-mindedly.

"As I see it, I have two problems," Walter said. "One of them is Jeremy, and the other one is Stilton."

She honored him with a period of silence. Sometimes he needed time to think.

"Which one do you want to start with?" she asked.

Walter sighed in resignation. He looked up and made eye contact with her.

"Let's start with my kid. He's a fuck-up, but he is *my* fuck-up. We can't change what he did, but we can influence the outcome. The public defender's office will assign him a burn-out or a doofus with pimples who hasn't even found the bathroom yet. That's just not good enough."

Walter considered his options. There were damn few.

"Ask legal to get me the best criminal lawyer in town, but let's keep it outside the company."

"Okay," she said. "I'll take care of it."

Walter studied the floor again.

"What about Stilton?" she asked.

Walter sighed. He glanced up at her and then looked back down at the floor.

"He needs to have an accident," Walter said.

He waited. They both knew what was coming.

"How do you propose to approach that?" she asked.

Walter shrugged. He needed the kind of help only she could arrange.

"I'm not sure," he said. "I don't want to leave a trail. You have any ideas?"

Walter studied her face. They both knew what he meant.

"Let me call some friends of mine on the south side," she said. "I'll see what they think."

CHAPTER THIRTY-NINE

Red Tie

Monday, May 2, 1977

For Italian food, the best place in town was Giorno's on the Hill. The man in the back corner wearing a shiny suit and red tie was enjoying his Bucatini con Guanciale Saporito. He didn't want to be disturbed right now. When he saw the guy coming his way, he took another bite and stared him down like a lion warning off a jackal. The intruder nodded and raised his hand and then took a seat at the bar to wait. He would simply have a beer and let the man enjoy his meal.

Red Tie mopped up his plate with a piece of garlic bread. He took a sip of wine and finally motioned the jackal over to the table.

"Whatcha got?" he asked as the guy sat down opposite him.

"It's a matter of professional courtesy. I'm here to ask a favor for a friend. A guy I know wants a grease ball done out in the soybeans. Seems a certain lawyer got into the drug business without knowing what he was doing and dragged my friend's kid into it. Cops bust it up, and the shyster makes like a rabbit, leaving the kid hanging. It's important he goes. You know anybody who might find this guy and help my friend out?"

Red Tie leaned back and considered the proposition. He pressed his fingertips together and pursed his lips.

"Maybe. Maybe not," he said. "Is this a business deal or personal?"

"My friend can handle the fare, no problem," said the jackal. "For you, it's business. For him, it's personal, if you know what I mean."

"Maybe we can work something out," said the man with the red tie. "Where?"

"Raleigh, middle of the state," said the jackal.

"I know the place," replied Red Tie. "Who's the target?"

"Guy named Stilton. Garrett Stilton. He's a gimp. People call him Tiltin' Stilton," said the jackal. "A lousy lawyer and a worse criminal. He's the kinda guy gives us all a bad name."

Red Tie absorbed this information.

"So he skipped town?" he asked.

"Yeah. Two, maybe three days ago," said the jackal. "He left in a hurry, so he probably left a trail."

Red Tie crossed his legs and poured the rest of the carafe of wine into his glass. Then he swirled it around before swigging it all down.

"I got a guy could do something on that. Say ten bills, unless it gets complicated," he said.

"Sounds reasonable," the jackal said.

"I need half to get things going. Half when it's done. That's how it works. We go nowhere until we see the front end."

"I came prepared."

"Give it to the barkeep," said Red Tie, "and tell him I said put it in the drawer. If the count is right, I'll send a guy tomorrow. If it ain't, I'll come looking for you."

Red Tie lowered a cold gaze on the jackal, and there was no question what he meant.

"Pleasure doin' business with you, as always," said the jackal. "You're a man people in need can turn to."

He reached out to shake on the deal. Red Tie took his hand.

"Write down all you got on this guy," he said, "And put it in the drawer with the front half."

"I can do that. Thank you."

"Don't thank me. It's just business. I'll let you know when the job's done."

Red Tie could smell the man's fear. Good. That's the way he liked to keep things.

He watched the jackal start backing away, watching his back on the way out of the room.

"I'm good with that. You know me. I go along," the jackal said, showing both palms.

Red Tie sighed in disgust.

"Look, I ain't gonna kiss you or nothin' like that, so go on. Get outta here and let me enjoy my dessert."

"I'm leaving now."

"So go. Go!" said Red Tie, shooing the jackal away from the table.

"I'm going."

For a whole lot of reasons, the jackal backed out of the restaurant with his hands in the air. Then he wheeled and disappeared from sight.

"Some people," Red Tie said.

He decided on tiramisu.

CHAPTER FORTY

The Yogurt Connection

Monday, May 2, 1977

If Linda Leary knew anything, it was how to compartmentalize her life. This hour belonged to politics. The half-hour slot afterwards belonged to business. For now, it would just have to wait.

All the fine ladies in the room recognized the president of the Indiana League of Woman Voters. She carried herself regally as she entered the tea room. Her black tailored skirt made her blue silk blouse pop. Her tiny diamonds and perfectly coiffed silver hair announced that she was a lady of wealth and power. As she performed with all the charm of a beloved queen, not one of her subjects would guess that moments ago she had received distressing news.

When the murmur subsided in the room, she turned and walked gracefully to the podium. She stood beside it, not behind it. She stood on her own for everyone to see. She needed nothing to lean on. She did not even need the microphone. With a clear, musical voice, she knew how to make her thoughts heard without amplification.

"Good afternoon, ladies. Thank you for being here. How are you?"

She received a warm round of applause.

"More important," she shouted, "how is Indiana?"

She paused before raising her voice, getting the timing just right.

"And most of all," she shouted, "what are we going to do about it?"

The audience reaction brought tears to her eyes.

At 3:45, her son, Paul Heilbrunn, opened the car door and slipped in beside her to talk.

"Well, how much did we lose?" she asked.

"A hundred and sixty kilos," Paul answered. "Frankly, I was afraid of this. Those outsiders who came to us at Christmas fumbled the play. A plane goes down in weather, the cops pick up that Bryce kid, and Stilton vanishes. The kid can hurt us, but that lawyer can kill us."

Linda Leary considered this in silence. She smoothed her skirt in the back of the limousine. Sometimes you have to protect what you have created.

"So we prune the tree," she said.

"Okay, Mom. I'll take care of it. See you later for dinner?"

"I'm looking forward to it," she answered.

Paul leaned over and kissed his mother on the cheek.

"I love you," he said. "Have a wonderful afternoon."

"Love you, too," she replied. "Tell Bonnie I said hello."

CHAPTER FORTY-ONE

Find Stilton

Tuesday, May 3, 1977

Paul Heilbrunn picked up the phone on his desk and called one of their guys who worked the enforcement angle. He rested his left ankle on his right knee.

"When can you come see me?" he asked. "I got some business to get done two states over."

He pulled one steel ball out and let it go, watching the one at the other end of the stack pop out and swing back. He always wondered how it knew.

"You tied up at the moment?" asked the guy they called Blondie.

"I have things I can do until you get here," Paul said. He was lying.

"Half hour, forty-five minutes okay?" asked Blondie.

"Yeah, fine. When you arrive, come on in. I'll tell Sally to expect you," said Paul.

"I'm on my way."

Sometimes it became necessary to prune the vines. Money disappeared, product disappeared. So the folks involved disappeared. When things got too loose, they quietly trimmed the branches. It kept everybody honest.

Paul glanced at his watch when Blondie arrived. Right on time. Paul was always amazed. The nearest ocean was eight hundred miles away, but Blondie still liked the surfer look. He wore blue jeans and a black Grateful Dead T-shirt. With sunglasses perched on his forehead,

182

he even had highlights in his shaggy hair. Blondie maintained a tan because it went over well with the ladies.

"I got another clean-up for you," Paul said. "A guy in Raleigh, Missouri, has to go. Garrett Stilton. He's an opportunist, so he got into our business. One little plane crash and his whole operation falls apart. He knows too much about us to leave him out there. Can you do this?"

"Yeah. I can take it on," Blondie said. "When?"

"Today," Paul answered. "The clock is ticking. Go pick up his trail, do it, and get back. Any questions?"

Paul waited for Blondie's answer.

"Lots. But I need to ask them somewhere else. Let me pack my socks and I'm gone. Highway 70 all the way?"

"Yeah, except for the last dozen miles or so. Check your map. Find him and fix it. Okay?"

"Gotcha."

CHAPTER FORTY-TWO

Melanie's Tale

Tuesday, May 3, 1977

Bud drove into the dump unannounced and parked near the office. He had some loose ends he needed to tie up. Melanie wasn't at the desk in front. Instead, she was sitting in Junior's old office with the door open.

He walked to the office door and leaned against the door frame.

"Hello, Melanie. Thought I'd come by to see how you were doing," Bud said. "You making it all right?"

"I guess that all depends on what you mean," she answered. "Business is okay. I was already running the place."

"I understand. So how about you? How are you holding up?"

"I have good days and bad days. This is a good day, so far."

"Grandpa doing okay?" Bud asked.

"Not worth a damn, frankly," she said. "He's been all screwed up since Junior died. He stays drunk as much as he can. It's better that way. When he's sober, can't nobody stand him. He's a mess, and his health ain't too good to start with."

"Sorry to hear that. Tell him I said hello."

"He'll be thrilled," she said.

She blew a bubble.

"I'm sure. Say, Melanie, do you mind if I ask a few questions about Junior's death?" Bud asked.

"I figured that was why you walked in here. Go ahead."

"The medical examiner said Junior was a bleeder," Bud said. "He had a high concentration of a blood thinner used in rat poison. Do you guys have a rat problem around here?"

"You ever see a garbage dump that didn't?"

"So, you use a lot of rat poison," Bud said.

"Some offices have a supply room full of pencils and paper," Melanie answered. "Come look at ours."

Bud followed her through a short hallway into a small room with old metal storage cabinets lining the walls. She opened the first one. It was full of rat traps and cardboard boxes of poison.

"We've had a hell of a time keeping them out of the office. The best way is not to bring food in here. Plus we keep traps and poison set all around the building. It's a never-ending battle."

Bud thought about that.

"You have any idea how Junior might have been exposed to it?" Bud asked. "Doc says he would have to ingest it often over a week or more to get levels that high."

"Ingest?"

"Swallow it. Inhale it. Get it on his skin."

"Like put out poison," she said, "and eat a sandwich without washing your hands?"

"That's one way, I suppose," said Bud. "Can you think of any others?"

"Look, it's probably not news to you that Junior had a drinking problem. He was drunk most of the time he was out here. I have no idea what he did when my back was turned, and I tried to keep it turned most of the time. He was a jerk. Stick a gun in my face, and see what happens. I just let him alone as much as I could. That, and run him off."

"Do you remember telling me that if I didn't act soon, you were gonna have to do it?" asked Bud.

"Yeah, and I meant it, too," Melanie said. "But then he died. I don't mean to sound cold or nothing, but some folks just need killing. Junior was one of 'em. Fortunately, somebody else thought so too."

"We're not gonna get anywhere with this are we, Melanie?"

"No, we ain't."

"Okay," Bud said. "So do you know how to drive that dozer out there?"

"I can start it, drive it across the dump, and shut it down," Melanie said. "But I ain't near good enough to park it on top of somebody in the dark."

"Any idea who is?"

"Yeah, most of the guys out here. They all fill in. Harlan, Jesse, Boone, even Pops."

"Who do you think hated Junior enough to run a Caterpillar up his pant legs?" Bud asked.

"Same list. Harlan, Jesse, Boone, Pops. Tell you the truth, I wish it'd been me."

Bud considered that for a moment.

"If you had to bet on it," he asked, "who would you put your money on?"

"Bud, they'd all line up to draw straws for the chance. I'm guessing it'd be the guy who got the longest straw."

"Well, just so you know, the medical examiner has made a determination on the cause and manner of death."

"Okay."

"Junior died because he bled to death."

"Surprise, surprise."

"There's more. Poisoning was a contributing factor, but not the direct cause of his death."

"Yeah, so what about the stabbing?" she asked.

"That was a contributing factor," he answered, "but those wounds may have been survivable. The thing that killed Junior was parking the dozer on him. He would have bled to death from that alone, but the critical thing is that he couldn't get help."

"You mean, find the driver and you found the killer?" Melanie asked.

"In so many words, yes."

"Sorry I can't help you with that."

"I thought so. Melanie, thank you for the information you provided. I understand why you were willing to take the chance."

"Meaning?"

"Meaning, I hope this is a new start for you. You won't have to live in fear any more. I hope you are up to that."

"Me too."

"See you."

"Bye."

Bud didn't really understand it, but his eyes watered as he was driving away.

CHAPTER FORTY-THREE

The Amateur Fugitive

Tuesday, May 3, 1977

Garrett rushed around, cramming money, clothes, and anything else he could grab into suitcases, boxes, and grocery sacks. He was getting the hell out of Dodge. Panicked? You could say that. The plane had crashed, and Jeremy was sitting in jail. It was just a matter of time before the kid squealed.

He decided against making a long-distance run for it. He figured the description of his car and the license plate number would be posted all over the Midwest. Instead, he went into hiding not far from home, without benefit of a plan.

He holed up in a farmhouse about ten miles outside of Claremont— part of an estate case. It was vacant, isolated, and he had a key. It never occurred to him that there would be no utilities or running water to flush the toilets. Even the kitchen stove was useless. The propane company had pulled the tank.

Garret left town rolling in dough but without a plan. He discovered hiding out was not as easy as it sounded. He went out at night searching for water and snacks, mostly hitting gas stations.

Stilton took the license plate off his car. He hit a lot of fast food restaurants until he discovered an all-night grocery. A week since his last a shower, he went to Wal-Mart to clean up and get toiletries and new clothing.

He intended to dash in and dash out, but the camping supply section mystified him. He had to decide not only on what he needed, but also learn how to use it. An hour later, he breathed a sigh of relief when he started his car. No one had stopped him. No one seemed to be watching his car. He was beginning to feel hopeful. Besides, he finally had a plan.

The guy who inherited the farm Stilton was using for a hideout lived in California. He had been adamant that he was never moving back to the farm.

"Sell it," he had told Stilton.

Garrett could find no buyers. Until now.

He drove in darkness from Wal-Mart back to Raleigh. He parked in an alley close to his office and slipped inside. When he came back out, he was carrying a manual typewriter, a ream of paper, and an example of a quit-claim deed.

When he finished drawing up the documents, he hauled his money up into the attic of the house and drove to the pay phone at a nearby gas station. Although phone booths always made him feel claustrophobic, he pulled the door closed.

"Mr. Dansig, this is Garrett Stilton, the lawyer for your mother's estate. I think I have found a buyer for the farm."

"At last. What did they offer?" said the voice on the other end of the line.

"One hundred eighty-five thousand," said Stilton.

"That's all?"

"In cash."

"Really?"

"Yes. And this particular buyer is rather impatient," added Stilton.

"Who is it?"

"Me, Mr. Dansig. That's all the money I have. I thought about it a lot, and I think it will make an excellent weekend retreat. When I finish refurbishing it, it can be my retirement home. It has been neglected for a long time now, but I think it has promise."

"So how would this work exactly?"

"Usually, when a buyer makes an offer, we have to mail the paperwork back and forth. You know, offer, counter-offer, like that.

As you can imagine, negotiating terms long distance can take a lot of time. Even then, you would still have to travel here to sign closing papers."

"So what are you getting at?" asked Dansig.

"I realize how inconvenient all this could be for you. I am willing to make it simple. If I buy the ticket, can you fly into St. Louis this Sunday for an hour or so, and fly home again with the money?"

"Hmm, yeah, I think so," Dansig said. "But I'm still not sure I understand."

"My idea is something called a quit-claim deed. I hand you the money, you sign one piece of paper, and I take care of the details. Essentially, you relinquish all property claims to me. I get the property as-is, without inspections, guarantees, or proof of clear title. You take the money, and I take the risk. Does putting cash in the bank Monday morning sound okay to you?"

"I'm thinking about it. Go on."

"I will waive all attorney fees for your mother's estate, just to prove that I have your best interests at heart."

"You've got a deal," said Dansig

"Okay. Let me call a travel agent. I'll call you again with the flight information. You can get the tickets at the counter. Will you be at this number for the next hour or so?"

"I have to run some errands. Can you give me a couple of hours?"

"Perfect," Stilton said. "I'll call you back two hours from now. Congratulations, Mr. Dansig, on settling your mother's estate. And clearing a tidy bundle in the process."

"Thanks. I'll expect to hear from you," Dansig said.

Now Garrett was really sweating. He had to decide whether to use a credit card or pay cash. Which would raise the least suspicion? He decided a phone call with a credit card would draw the least attention. By the time the credit card purchase came to someone's attention, he would be gone, and the sale would be a matter of record.

Without any distractions, he spent a lot of time thinking. Sooner or later he was going to get caught. That would mean conspiracy to distribute marijuana. A conviction could get him anything from five to forty years. But he never touched the product, and it would come down to his word against Dewey's. On the other side, it would be his word against Jeremy's. A good lawyer could cast sufficient doubt to get him off.

Meanwhile, he had two good hands to play when it came to plea bargaining. He could give up the Indianapolis outfit, and he could give up Walter Bryce's blackmail scheme. That stuff had to be worth something.

Still, something nagged him. He was a sitting duck out at the farm. If he turned himself in, he could say he was cooperating, and get off the streets. After a week on the run, that started to sound pretty good. All this solitude out in the godforsaken country was making him crazy.

That's what led to his little scheme. Store the money in the attic, buy the farm from Dansig with a quit-claim deed, and go to the county courthouse on Monday morning to file the deed. Once the property was his, he could go to the sheriff's office and turn himself in.

So all he had to do was hang on until Sunday and make a round trip to St. Louis. Maybe two week's time made the description of his car a distant memory.

If he could remain calm, $993,000 would be his. What's more, he had time to decide how to use it. The thought of almost being a millionaire was a comfort to him. He would stall his way through the system to increase his credit for time served. At least there wouldn't be snakes, chiggers, and rats.

CHAPTER FORTY-FOUR

The Last Petiole

Wednesday, May 4, 1977

Bud took the list of people who knew how to drive the D-3 Caterpillar to the office. His deputies could check out their alibis. The one who troubled him most was old man Petiole. He claimed to be drunk at the time. Witnesses confirmed it. But no one could account for his whereabouts later that night. Bud didn't like it. Still, he had a hard time imagining Pops doing such a thing.

Melanie's call came unexpectedly.

"Bud, what happens when a suspect has a stroke?"

"Whoa, Melanie. That question covers a lot of ground. What's the crime? Speeding? Defacing public property? Assault with a deadly weapon? Who is it? How solid is the evidence? Is a prosecuting attorney really going to go after this person? How debilitating was the stroke? So maybe you should give me some particulars."

"Pops started talking gibberish this morning, none of the words fitting together. My cousin noticed his face sagging on one side, and he started having difficulty getting his words out. He seemed paralyzed on one side. She called an ambulance."

"Hmm. I see what you mean."

"What if he did it, Bud, and no one will ever know?"

"Melanie, not everything that happens in this lifetime is reconciled before we leave. What Pops is going through right now is really terrible. I am so sorry."

"It's pretty scary to think about running this business all alone."

"Melanie, you've been doing it for years. You remember what you said you always wanted to do out there?"

"Landscape?"

"Yeah. How did the rest of it go?"

"Just because this place is a dump doesn't mean it has to look like one." She laughed.

"Well, it looks like you got your chance."

"Thanks for listening to me, Bud."

"No problem."

"Bye." Click. She was gone.

Bud hung up his phone and sat, lost in thought. Melanie had just implicated her grandfather to ease her own guilt, yet he didn't mind it that much. What troubled him was that he let her do it.

He had taken an oath to uphold the law, but he just finished comforting a woman he suspected of attempting murder. Someone else just got there ahead of her. Still, he felt compassion for them all. He even felt compassion for Junior, even though he was worthless.

Bud sat back in his chair and put his feet up on the desk. When crimes get committed, the criminals are people first. Despite everything that happens, they still are people. Bud shook his head. He couldn't tell the guilty and innocent apart any more.

CHAPTER FORTY-FIVE

Guilt and Innocence

Wednesday, May 4, 1977

That evening at Lucy's house, Bud told her about Melanie's call. They were listening to music in her living room. He was on the end of the couch, and she was curled up against him.

"I must be getting soft."

"Why?"

"I don't think we'll ever find enough evidence to prosecute Melanie or old man Petiole for what they did to Junior, and frankly, I don't mind it. Their whole family is like one big Greek tragedy. They live in a hell of their own making. So maybe I'm not fit for this job anymore."

Lucy sat up and looked at him.

"So, are you going to pack it in and let Tiltin' Stilton go?" she asked.

"No. Him I'm going to find and hold accountable."

"So why the difference?"

"That's what baffles me," Bud said. "Somehow, Melanie feels innocent to me. I don't mean innocent of a crime. I mean a certain childlike innocence inside her. Her life has been hell, and she had to fight to survive. Almost like self defense."

Lucy did something she frequently did at times like this. She kicked off her shoes, pulled her legs up on the couch, and tucked her feet between the cushions. Bud considered it a tell. It meant she thought "this is important, and I'm not going anywhere until we are finished." He loved her for it.

"So tell me," she said, "do you find any innocence in a father who would run over his own son with a bulldozer. I'd call that parental disapproval, wouldn't you?"

"Lucy, I've asked myself just how angry I would have to be to crush a man like that and leave him to die. I'm guessing the old man unleashed a lifetime of anger and disappointment, but this time he wanted to make sure Junior got the message."

Bud reflected on that for a while. Then he turned to look Lucy in the eye.

"So, no, I don't find the same kind of innocence in him that I do in Melanie. Still, he never struck me as a man who was evil by nature."

"How about Stilton?" Lucy asked.

"I have never met anyone with such a black heart. People marry each other because the bond is so strong they never want to be apart. So how sick do you have to be to torture your own loved one with clamps and needles?"

"And burning cigarettes. It's not love. It's control," Lucy said.

"I consider Stilton inherently evil. It's not like he made a mistake in the heat of passion. Everything he does is self-serving. He takes advantage of the weak and vulnerable, like Clyde Dewey and Jeremy Bryce," Bud said.

Bud felt Lucy lean against him again, filling in all the hollow places. She teased him, twirling a finger against his chest while pretending to ask a child-like question.

"So, Sheriff, do you ignore a crime because the perp has an innocent spirit, and only go after those you despise as truly wicked?"

"No. That judgment belongs to the court. I have to take them as I find them. It's just that, in some cases, I find them more easily than others."

"Tell me, what's wrong with that?" Lucy asked.

"It means I am not as impartial as I should be."

He felt Lucy's eyes on him. When he turned to look at her, she kissed him. Then she sank back down in his arms again.

"I think it means you are human. Even a sheriff has emotions. At least you pay attention to yours. Bud, you are good at what you do because you care about people: the ones you work with, the crime victims, the ones you bust, the ones you send away. You do your job; still you care. I don't see it as a weakness."

He pulled her closer. She put her head on his chest. He kept his arms around her and just held on.

CHAPTER FORTY-SIX

You Get What You Pay For

Thursday, May 5, 1977

Bud sat with his feet propped on his desk as he thumbed through the file on Jeremy Bryce. When the high-dollar lawyer out of St. Louis learned Andy Russell's logbook matched their clandestine photos of his client, he started fishing for a plea bargain.

Jeremy either had a very fertile imagination or there was something extraordinary afoot in Indianapolis. When Bud called the Indy Police Department, he hit a brick wall. They didn't want to talk to him.

Lucy saw through it. If Jeremy's claims were true, some big dogs could be in on the hunt. The DEA had a reputation for protecting undercover agents. Helping a back-country sheriff was a good way to start springing leaks.

Bud's problem was that the local prosecutor didn't buy Jeremy's story. He asked Bud to check it out. Since Indianapolis wouldn't cooperate, Bud had a problem. He needed a tunnel rat, someone who could go in, gather intelligence, and get out without being seen. He called Raymond.

When Raymond arrived at the office, Bud went out to meet him. Then he led him back to his desk. Raymond looked jumpy when he closed the door, so Bud turned a chair around backwards, straddled it and sat down facing him. He leaned forward, arms resting on the back of the chair.

"Ray, what I am about to tell you must remain between us. You can't tell another living soul. Are you in or out?"

197

"Oh, well hey. Thanks for giving me enough information to make an informed choice," Raymond said.

"This is no bullshit," Bud said. "We've been through a lot together. Not just good times. There were times I threw you in jail. I'm not banking on friendship here. This is all about trust. I need to know if we can trust each other."

Bud took a deep breath and let it out. He studied Raymond's eyes as they flitted around the room. He watched the tiny twitches in his facial expressions.

"What is this about?" Raymond asked.

Bud made eye contact with him and held it.

"It's about going into unknown territory, collecting solid intelligence, and bringing it back to me, all without leaving any footprints."

Raymond crossed his arms and thought.

"I guess I'd have to be pretty stupid not to see that you're baiting me. Make me curious so I will say yes," he said.

"You don't have to say yes. This isn't 'Nam."

Bud watched Raymond's eyes. He spotted the decision before it was announced.

"If I'm going to have a big adventure, you'd better fill me in."

Bud relaxed. So did Raymond.

"I'll give you the succinct version and then answer your questions," Bud said.

"When have you ever done it any other way?"

Bud lifted one hand and pushed his glasses back onto his nose.

"Jeremy Bryce says there is a huge marijuana supply network based in Indianapolis. Andy Russell was flying the stuff in for them at night."

"Okay," Raymond said.

"Jeremy says it is headed up by a wealthy socialite named Linda Leary, and her two sons, Richard and Paul Heilbrunn," Bud continued. "Supposedly, she is above suspicion, president of the Indiana League of Women Voters, and owns a chain of yogurt stores."

"Nice."

"They claim to be selling soap, but it is just a cover for the dope network," Bud said. "Here's the problem. The kid's lawyer wants to plea bargain, but the prosecutor doesn't believe the story. He says it sounds like a fairy tale."

"I can understand that," Raymond said.

"I called the Indy PD, but they weren't talking. At first, I wondered if the guy I talked to was dirty. Then Lucy says, 'What if it's true?' A big undercover operation, like the DEA, could be underway. A case like that takes years, so they have to keep it under wraps."

"So what do you want me to do?"

"Go there, find out if there really is a Linda Leary and sons, and confirm as much of Jeremy's story as possible. Presuming there is a joint taskforce investigation, you have to slip in and out without being seen, blowing their cover or stepping on any landmines. That's all."

"That's it, huh?" Raymond said. "No big deal, right. So, what's in it for me?"

Bud leaned back and smiled.

"You're the investigative journalist. At some point this will become a scoop. You tell me."

Raymond thought in silence for quite a while, his fingertips resting on his chin.

"I know how to do it," he said.

"How?"

"Ride the Harley. No one pays attention to a crazy Vietnam vet on a hog."

"Good cover," Bud said. "When can you go?"

"As soon as I know everything you know," Raymond said.

"Let me get the details together for you. Lunchtime tomorrow?"

"That'll be good. Dutch's?"

"You're buying," said Bud.

"Yeah, right. Better cash in while you can."

Thirty minutes later, Cassius Greene rapped on Bud's open door. Bud looked up and invited him in.

"What have you got, Cassius?"

"Thought you'd want to know what we found in Junior's car."

"Okay, let's hear it."

"The autopsy report says Junior's blood type was A negative. There were pools of it in the front passenger seat. It matches the blood trail from the car to the body. The handprint on the hood came back O negative, and the blood from the steering wheel is A positive. We have three bleeders in the car."

"You sure?"

"Solid forensics."

"Interesting. Is Clyde Dewey in the mix anywhere?"

"No. His blood type is B-something. But he wasn't one of them." He paged through his notes until he found what he was looking for. "Clyde is a B negative."

"So walk me through the scenario the way you see it."

"Okay, but there is some stuff you need to hear first," Cassius said.

"Shoot."

"Two guys claiming to be Eddie and Bobby Smith show up in the emergency room at University Hospital in Claremont just a few hours after Junior died. Both had scalp and head injuries requiring stitches and X-rays. They said they were pistol whipped outside a bar. One of them had a concussion, and the other had shattered bones under his left eye.

"The ER folks say the injuries matched what they described, but neither one of them had been drinking. No boozy smell. Blood alcohol tests negative. One of them was typed O negative and the other was A positive—same as in the car."

"What have we got for ID on these guys?"

"Nothing. They called somebody to cover the hospital bill. The check arrived last week, signed by Garrett R. Stilton."

"Really! Isn't that interesting? So how do you see it?" asked Bud.

"Let's start at the Blue-Belle Cleaners," Cassius said. "Dewey stabs Junior when he pulls a gun. Junior drops the gun and grabs the broom handle. Clyde gets the gun and runs Junior out. Junior begs for his piece, Clyde unloads it, and tosses it into the alley to get him to go away. Clyde stashes the bullets in a can of muck from his machines, and produces them later on."

"Okay, so how do we get Junior to the dump?" Bud asked.

"Junior has an empty gun and a bad gut wound. I see these guys jumping him in town and driving him out to the dump, maybe to kill him, I don't know. But he pistol-whips them so bad they run for it, taking his car."

"Were there any prints or blood on the dozer?"

"No. Driver either wore gloves or did a wipe-down after."

"If my count is right, we've got five people trying to kill Junior," said Bud.

"What can I say? Looks like Junior had a bad night."

"That's hard to believe."

"Look at the evidence: one, poison; two, stabbed with a stick; three and four, two John Does get their heads cracked; five, somebody parks a dozer on him."

"And six, Stilton covers the hospital bills. Hit men, you think?"

"That's my guess."

"They must have been amateurs. They jump a guy who is drunk, gored, and out of bullets, and he still beats the crap out of them," said Bud.

"That's how I see it."

"Sounds like Stilton cutting corners. Okay, Cassius. Nice work. Take it to Sam and Kuhlmann. Let's see if anyone else has any other ideas. So, will we ever catch the Smith brothers?"

"Fingerprints may turn up. I'm working on that now, but it's slow."

"Stay on it, but concentrate on Stilton. We need solid forensics in court."

"That's what I thought you'd say. I'll keep digging."

Sheriff Bud got his usual booth at Dutch's and waited for Raymond. When he showed up, Bud handed him some papers.

"Memorize this between here and Indianapolis," he said. "Don't take it in with you."

"Yeah. That could be awkward."

Then Bud filled Raymond in on Junior's last hours. Bud saw Raymond's eyebrows go up.

"So how do you score this on the credibility scale?" Raymond asked.

"It's so damned unbelievable I have to rate it pretty high, for two reasons."

"What?" Raymond asked.

"It is too bizarre to be made up," Bud said. "The second is the forensics."

"Uh huh."

"What?"

"I'd say, under the circumstances, Junior gave a pretty good account of himself," Raymond said.

"What do you mean?"

"Poisoned and speared, he still runs off two goons," answered Ray. "Even when he's sitting on the ground bleeding to death, someone decides to squash him to make sure he dies. That's one tough bastard."

"A soldier's perspective?"

"Yeah. It still doesn't make him a nice guy, though, does it?" asked Raymond.

"That seems to be the consensus."

They ate in silence for a few minutes. Bud picked up his coffee mug and took a sip. His fingertips drummed on it while he thought.

"Let me ask you a question," Bud said, pushing his plate aside.

"What is it?"

"If you were Stilton, where would you go? Think like him for a minute," said Bud.

"The first thing that comes to mind is to get as far away from here as possible."

"Without planes, trains, or buses, that means a road trip," Bud said. "State troopers haven't seen him. What does that say to you?"

"He's here?"

"But where?" asked Bud.

"If he hasn't been seen in Raleigh, what are his other options?" Raymond asked. "Claremont?"

Bud shrugged.

"I don't know, but I don't think he's an outdoorsman, do you?"

"That's a really interesting question you've got there."

"Thank you."

A stranger wearing a red tie and a shiny suit rose from the booth behind them. He walked to the cash register to place his check and a twenty dollar bill on the counter, and then quietly slipped out the door.

CHAPTER FORTY-SEVEN

The Trip to Lambert

Sunday, May 8, 1977

Garrett Stilton's shoes were a mess, but it was too late now. He'd try to hit the shoe shine stand before he met the plane. He couldn't expect to be successful looking shabby, so he left in time to go by Wal-Mart to look for a blazer or a jacket. He found a black turtleneck and a leather jacket that looked good on him. After a short stop to gas up and run through a hamburger stand, he was on his way.

Rather than run the risk of being pulled over by a state trooper for not having a tag on the car, Garrett put it back on. When he got onto I-70, he cruised at the speed limit and stayed in the middle of the traffic. He just wanted to blend in.

He watched for police cars, but the guy in a brown two-toned Dodge Charger who passed him seemed awfully curious. Then he disappeared into the traffic behind him, probably a false alarm.

Garrett drove to Lambert-St. Louis Airport, and into the terminal. He carried only a leather briefcase and bypassed the ticket counters. He didn't notice the guy from the Charger following him.

Garrett headed down Concourse B to gate twenty-six. The sign over the counter said TWA Flight 604 arriving from Denver. When the plane pulled up to the jet way, Garrett rose. He stepped into the middle of the concourse and stood where he could see the arriving passengers. He hailed a man traveling alone and led him to a low bank of telephone booths. He motioned for the guy to sit down, and used the booth for a temporary office. He handed the briefcase to the guy and then pulled a pen and paper out of his pocket. The traveler signed the paper, and Garrett put it back in his pocket.

The traveler stood up and looked at his ticket for a gate number. The lawyer pointed him down the concourse. They departed with a wave, and Garrett headed back to his car.

He didn't see the driver of the Charger flip down his sunglasses and pull out into traffic behind him. Garrett glanced in his rearview mirror. He felt pretty smug. The filing at the court house would be easy. Once his money was safe, he could run damage control while he worked his way through the legal system. He didn't have to live like a wild animal any more. In a few years, he would be free. And rich.

Garrett pulled down the visor. The late afternoon sun blazed in through the windshield. He hadn't felt this good in a long time. He didn't know the names of the flowers alongside the road, but he enjoyed the colors just the same. The air smelled crisp, and he was beginning to appreciate the smell of the earth. This had been a good day.

He turned left onto the final stretch and saw the two-story white farmhouse up ahead. It looked rundown, but he would find someone to fix it up for him. Right now, it was the first hopeful thing he had ever known in his life. He slowed down to enjoy the view. He realized his property line came all the way to the corner of this pasture.

CHAPTER FORTY-EIGHT

Count Your Enemies

Sunday, May 8, 1977

One of the nice things about Red Tie's job was that he didn't have to follow the rules. Breaking and entering was just a part of his line of work. He was in Stilton's office less than an hour when he ran across the registration papers for a 1972 Lincoln. Shortly afterward, he found the file on the Dansig estate, located just outside Claremont.

When Red Tie explored Stilton's hideout, he realized the man lived like a pig. Trash was piled high in one corner, dirty clothes in another. What's more, all the shopping bags were from Wal-Mart. If this was how this guy chose to live, Red Tie could honestly say he was about to perform a public service. Now that he found the lawyer's lair, he would be patient.

Determining which way Stilton would return was fairly easy. In one direction, the gravel road ran down into fields along the river bottom. The other way led to town.

He noticed an open gate and a driveway leading to a barn. Tall brush had grown up along both sides of the gravel lane. That would serve for an ambush. Red Tie backed his Grand Marquis into the lane and waited. He listened to classical music on the radio. He loved Vivaldi. He had a glorious afternoon. He even got to hear all of Respighi's "Pines of Rome."

When the sun swung low in the horizon, Red Tie turned off the radio, started the engine, and sat up to study the crest of the hill. He watched for a cloud of dust coming his way. When it arrived, he had plenty of time to ID the Lincoln.

Alternately hitting the throttle and the brake, he lurched out onto the gravel road and stopped, blocking both lanes. He popped the hood release and stepped out. The Lincoln fishtailed to a stop as he lifted the hood. The driver of the Lincoln lowered the window and stuck his head out.

"Got a problem?" called the driver.

Red Tie wiped his hands with a handkerchief and stepped away from the hood. He smiled and walked toward the Lincoln.

"Damn thing just quit on me. I'm not much of a mechanic. How about you?"

"Wish I could help you, but I don't know anything about …"

Red Tie pulled his revolver and aimed it at Stilton.

"You Garrett Stilton?"

"Yeah, but who the hell are you? What do you want? Money? I got money."

"A friend of mine wants you dead. This ain't personal. It's just business."

Red Tie jumped when a brown Dodge Charger punched through the plume of dust and swerved into a stop behind Stilton. The driver of the Charger bailed out and ran up alongside the passenger window of Stilton's car. He had a gun.

"Stop right there!" commanded Red Tie.

He aimed his gun at the blond man, who wheeled and pointed his gun at him.

"Who the fuck are you?" the blond man asked.

"I was just going to ask you the same question," Red Tie said.

"Listen, I've been tailing this jerk all day. When I decide it's time to pop him, you're standing there with a gun on him. What the hell is going on here?"

Red Tie stepped back.

"You were going to pop him? I was just getting ready to do it."

"Wait a minute. Wait a minute. Let's lower our guns and figure out what's going on here," said the man with blond hair.

He cautiously lowered his gun, and Red Tie followed suit.

Suddenly, Stilton stomped down hard on the gas pedal and crashed into Red Tie's car.

"I've been told to waste this guy," Blondie yelled.

Stilton yanked his car into reverse, spun the tires, and threw gravel as he backed into Blondie's car.

"My people sent me to kill him, too," Red Tie said.

"Are you a professional?" asked Blondie.

Red Tie spread both arms wide.

"Do I look like an amateur?"

Stilton jammed his car into gear, surging forward again into Red Tie's car.

Then he slammed it back into reverse.

"Let's do what we came here to do. We can chit chat later," Blondie said.

"Okay. On the count of three?" asked Red Tie.

"On three."

"One … two … three!"

Together they wheeled and fired through the windshield at Stilton. He bounced off the seat and fell forward onto the horn. It blared. Red Tie strolled casually to the open driver's window, grabbed Stilton by the hair, and pushed him over into the seat. The horn went silent. Red Tie reached in with his handkerchief and turned off the ignition.

"So what kind of gun do you use?" Blondie called out.

"This?" Red Tie said as he held up the revolver. "A Ruger SP101. Five rounds, 357 magnum, hollow points. What do you use?" He walked back toward the blond man.

"A Glock 17. Nine millimeters. How come you're still using a revolver? That's kind of old school, isn't it?"

"You'll understand when that piece of plastic shit jams on you during a job. Wheel guns don't jam."

"But only five rounds? Mine's got fourteen."

"Yeah? How many shots did you fire?"

"One. Same as you."

Red Tie stood with his hands on his hips.

"See? Whaddya say let's can the bullshit and get out of here?" he asked.

"Okay. See ya."

"You should get a real gun," Red Tie said.

"Maybe I will."

Blondie holstered his gun in the small of his back and turned to walk to his car. Red Tie raised his arms and shot Blondie between the shoulder blades. He pitched forward onto the hood of his car and slowly slid off onto the ground. A streak of red mapped his fall.

"Amateur," Red Tie said.

For years, he had followed a simple policy. Leave no witnesses and leave no brass. He stood patiently until he was certain both men were dead. Then he got in his car and left.

CHAPTER FORTY-NINE

Next County Over

Monday, May 9, 1977

Bud was studying payroll sheets, approving overtime for his deputies, when the phone rang. He picked it up.

"Oswald."

"Sheriff Oswald, this is Sheriff Dugan over in Claremont. You looking for a guy named Garrett Stilton?"

Bud put down the payroll sheets. He took off his glasses and pinched the bridge of his nose with his free hand.

"Yes."

"Well, you can stop looking. We got him shot dead over here in a Lincoln. Got another guy shot in the back. Looks like your case slopped over into Booker County. Can you come over and help me make some sense out of this mess?"

"On my way. Tell me how to find you."

Bud pulled up to the crime scene. Tape stretched across the road from fence to fence. He stepped out of his truck and took it all in. Beyond the distant string of tape sat two cruisers from Dugan's office. The ME's car and a hearse were pulled up close behind them.

Between the tapes, Stilton's Lincoln sat crooked on the gravel road, the headlights bashed out. The trunk rested against the side of a Dodge Charger, which sat crossways on the road. Bud noticed two bullet holes in the Lincoln's windshield less than three inches apart. All he could see of the driver over the dash was one shoulder.

Sheriff Dugan walked up and shoved his hat back on his head.

"Bud, thanks for coming out. According to his driver's license, Stilton's the guy in the front car there. His wallet's the only thing we pulled. We told the ME not to move him until you had a chance to see the scene. C'mon. Let me show you around."

They walked away from the road to cross the ditch. A path followed the fence line. Dugan led him until they were alongside Stilton's car. Both front doors were open, and Bud could see Stilton slumped over on the seat. He followed Dugan along the path to a place where they could see the second body lying by the front wheel of the Charger.

"Do you know that guy?" asked Dugan.

Bud studied the trim build, the sunglasses lying in the gravel, and the bleached blond hair.

"I don't recognize him. What have you got?"

"Nothing. No ID. No registration. Just Indiana plates. Guy's got a nine millimeter behind his back. We haven't processed any evidence yet, except for this."

Dugan held up a plastic bag with a nine millimeter shell casing in it.

Bud figured ballistics would match the shell and the gun.

"We found it over where that marker is. Haven't run across any others yet."

"Have your guys photographed everything?" Bud asked.

"Yeah, we done it while we was waiting for you."

Bud turned slowly to take in the whole scene from this vantage point. He took a deep breath and blew it out. He pointed to the body by the Charger.

"Okay. Then let's start with this guy," Bud said. "First let's find out if he fired his gun."

They crossed the ditch and stepped up onto the gravel road. Bud took out his ballpoint. Slipping it through the trigger guard, he pulled the gun free and lifted it to his nose to sniff the muzzle.

"It's been fired. Do you want to dump the magazine and count the rounds out here, or do you want to bag it and take it back to your lab?" he asked.

"Bud, our lab is my desk. Let me get one of my deputies to do it here."

"Okay, remember the finger prints on the gun and cartridges. He may have to dust it first."

"Right." Dugan took the pen and gun from Bud and carried it down the road to his crime scene guy.

Bud studied the bloody smear on the Charger. He could almost see the poor guy slamming face forward onto the hood before he slid off. Only a high-caliber hollow point could do that much damage.

"Looks like he hit the car face-first before he slid off onto the ground," said Dugan when he returned. "What do you think?"

"That's what it looked like to me," said Bud.

He knelt down to inspect the body.

"He took at least one round in the back. When you turn him over, the exit wound will be nasty. Looks like he may have taken one through the heart."

"That's some pretty good shooting," Dugan said.

"I was thinking the same thing," said Bud. "Let's let the ME start processing this guy."

"Okay."

Dugan waved the medical examiner toward them. He pointed to the body on the ground. The ME grabbed his kit and slipped under the tape.

"Let us know if he was shot more than once," Dugan said.

Then he turned to Bud.

"Want to go see what happened next-door?"

"Okay."

They turned to walk back toward the Lincoln. Dugan filled him in on the way.

"Two rounds went through the windshield."

"I saw that. Too low for a head shot, don't you think?"

"We didn't see any head trauma. I figure they was both torso shots."

Late in the day a flatbed hauled the last car away from the scene. The guy face down in the road had only fired a single round. Bud knew they were looking to identify two shooters. Identifying the guy shot in the back would be easier than figuring out who killed him. The medical examiner would have to tell them what happened to Stilton.

Bud had helped Dugan all he could today. It was time to wait for ballistics, autopsies, and trace evidence. But they both recognized the earmarks of a professional job.

On the way home, Bud realized Raleigh County got to close the Stilton case, but Booker County had two new homicides. Farm country just wasn't the same anymore. He thought about Sheriff Dugan. He was a new guy but learning fast. At least he knew when to ask for help with a double homicide. Bud could work with men like that.

CHAPTER FIFTY

Grammar Matters

Monday, June 6, 1977

Raymond Thornton rode back into Raleigh with a month's growth of beard and the story of a lifetime. It just happened to be one he could not publish. He went straight to Bud. The sheriff ushered him into the office and closed the door.

"Everything Jeremy Bryce said is true," Raymond said. "Linda Leary and her boys are so high-profile in that town that they were easy to find."

After riding all day, Raymond really didn't want to sit anymore. He paced the floor and told his story while Bud sat behind his desk with his feet up.

"The most amazing thing was the night freight ramp at Indianapolis International. The traffic for Federal Express and UPS provided perfect cover for the drug network," said Raymond. "Paul wears fancy suits and drives a BMW, and he is absolutely ruthless. People who cross him are known to disappear."

"Did you step on any toes while you were there?" Bud asked. "I sure don't want to torque up anybody's investigation."

"In 'Nam, there were times when I could feel snipers scoping me. I can't explain it. I just had this feeling. The same thing happened a couple of times in Indianapolis. I never saw them, but I'm pretty sure they saw me. I would do my best imitation of a guy who was just passing through."

"So what do I tell the prosecutor?" Bud asked.

Raymond crossed his arms and locked eyes with Bud.

"Tell him you can't verify any of it," Raymond answered.

Bud grunted and thought about that. Raymond watched him. When Bud's eyebrow cocked, Raymond explained.

"I think it's too early to let any of this get into the public record. People could get hurt."

Three days later, Raymond parked his pickup in front of the Grayson home. He rolled the windows down for Tracker, and told him to stay in the truck. Raymond closed the door and reached in through the window to scratch Tracker behind the ear. Then he turned and lifted a sealed box out of the bed of the truck. He tucked it under his arm and strolled up to the porch.

Before he could ring the doorbell, Meredith spotted him and ran to open the door.

Raymond knelt down to give her a hug and kiss her on the forehead. She grabbed him by the hand and pulled him inside.

"Mama," she called out. "Uncle Raymond is here!"

Raymond recognized the aroma of fresh cookies and bread in the oven. Betty Ann came out of the kitchen to greet him with a smile and a hug. With a sweep of a hand, she invited him to join her in the kitchen.

"I've got some coffee on. Would you like a cup?" she said.

"Sure. That would be nice."

He sat at the kitchen table and placed the box on the floor beside him.

Betty fetched Raymond a cup of coffee and joined him.

"What's in the box, Uncle Ray?" Meredith asked.

He reached down to pick it up and placed it on the table in front of him.

"This is something I want to give to your Mama for safekeeping," he said.

Across the top of it, he had written "Letters to Millie." Betty Ann looked at him through teary eyes and sniffed.

"What's this all about?" she asked.

"I have some good news," Raymond answered. "Lou Baxter is going to give me my old job back at the paper. I'm a reporter again."

Betty Ann cocked her head at him and smiled in that funny way that she had.

"You always were," she said. "So what's with the box?"

"It's simple, really. We can't undo tragedies, but we don't have to let them undo us. I don't want these to go away, but having them around the house is … well, it is hard. I thought you would understand and might be willing to keep them for me."

She wiped a tear off her cheek and smiled.

"I'm flattered that you trust me that much."

"I always have, Betty. I always have."

Raymond turned to put his arm around Meredith.

"I have something for you, too," he said.

"What is it?" Meredith asked.

"It is a secret between you and me and your mommy."

"What is it?"

"It is something you can go see for yourself when you get to high school," Raymond said. "Room 206 used to be Aunt Millie's old classroom. Go to her desk and pull out the center drawer. If you dig down to the bottom, you will see something Aunt Mille wrote there years ago."

"What does it say?"

"It says, 'Grammar matters. It proves you're educated.' She even signed it —Margaret Millicent McKenna."

CHAPTER FIFTY-ONE

The Well-Stone Writing Festival

Monday, June 13, 1977

Raymond watched people in Raleigh trying to get back to a normal life. Some had more success than others. He was amazed when Bud came to him for advice. The sheriff sat in Raymond's truck with him, Tracker curled up happily between them.

"I'm not sleeping worth a damn, Raymond, and I don't know what to do about it."

Bud was looking out the window. He wouldn't make eye contact.

"I'm not sure I understand," Raymond answered. "What's the problem?"

"Nightmares. If it's not that pilot, it's Junior Petiole, or Stilton, or the dead gunman rolling over to show me the hole in his chest. I wake up screaming, sweating, and gasping for breath. Lucy says to get counseling before it destroys our lives."

Raymond closed his eyes and thought about all his lost nights. He reached across the truck cab and gently tapped Bud's shoulder.

"Hey," he said. "Look at me."

Bud slowly turned to face him, no longer trying to check the tears welling up in he eyes.

"Here's the deal, partner," Raymond said. "What you have been through is called combat. It never goes away, but with time it loses leverage. So what you do is bury the dead by living. I don't know, maybe go dancing with Lucy. She is the best medicine you will ever find. Millie did that for me. Lucy can do that for you."

They sat together in silence for a long time. Finally, Bud leaned forward and began to straighten his uniform. Without a word, he opened the door and stepped down into the street. He closed the door and then pulled on his hat, tugging it into place. He leaned over to glance through the open window as he gave the door a couple of pats.

"Thanks, Ray. I believe I'll do that very thing."

Then he checked traffic and crossed the street. As Raymond watched him go he said a silent prayer. They never spoke of it again.

The annual Well-Stone writing festival was upon them. The name came from a remark Millie once made. She said writing was like tossing stones down a well. Sometimes you have to listen for the splash at the bottom to know whether it is any good.

To Raymond, it seemed like a lifetime ago when she encouraged him to write *A Soldier's Heart*. This year the festival organizers invited him to be a speaker and to describe how he came to write his book.

He didn't give it much thought until he read that hundreds of Vietnam vets were planning to ride their motorcycles to Raleigh just to hear him. These guys had been there, and they had tales of their own. Raymond felt apprehension for the first time in years. He didn't want to disappoint them.

At once, it brought everything back to him, but also offered a chance for many to put their burdens down. Raymond thought every day about his two buddies who made it back to the world with him only to commit suicide within six months. The heartbreak returned, but this time Millie was not here to help him through the rough patches.

The day before the festival, the whole gang had dinner at Dutch's Diner. Over the years, they learned the atmosphere at Dutch's changed during festival time. When their orders arrived, Wally blessed the food and they began to eat.

Out of the corner of his eye, Raymond noticed two Harleys pulling up to share a parking spot. Both bikes sported American flags, eagles, and sweethearts on the back. Two couples dismounted, took off their riding gear, and entered Dutch's Diner. Raymond recognized them as vets. He turned his attention back to his friends.

"Raymond, what day were you going to speak?" asked Betty Ann.

"Oh, Tuesday, 2:00 PM, at the Odd Fellows' Lodge. I understand it's been painted."

"Are we invited, or is this party for GIs only?"

He took a sip of coffee before he answered. He had to give that some thought.

"Well, Betty, some of the wives and girlfriends will be there, too, so I can't think of a reason why you wouldn't be welcome. It may be uncomfortable, but I could use a cheering section."

"I want to come, too," Meredith announced. Everyone turned to look at her. An awkward silence fell over the table.

"Um, honey," Betty Ann said, "I'm not sure this is the sort of thing young girls would enjoy. They will be talking about bad things that happened during the war."

"I know that, but the war is over now. When do we start talking about the good things that are going to happen?"

Wally stopped eating in mid-chew and put his club sandwich down. He shot a glance at Raymond and Bud. Then he looked into Betty Ann's eyes. They read each other for a moment.

"Sweetheart," he said to Meredith, "you make a very good point. We'll have to think about it."

It certainly gave Raymond a change of perspective.

Just as the mood at their table became light-hearted once again, one of the riders rose and approached their table.

"Excuse me," he said to Raymond, "are you the author who told our story?"

Raymond was speechless.

"If you're talking about *A Soldier's Heart*, I'm the one who put it on paper. The guys I served with actually wrote it."

The rider let out a big breath. His eyes watered.

"That's what I thought," he said, offering his hand. "Thank you."

Raymond shook his hand. A lot passed between them in that moment. Willie stared open-mouthed. He didn't know his uncle was famous. Meredith studied Lucy, who was smiling, and then looked around to read the rest of the adults around her.

"Do you mind if I introduce my wife and my friends?" the rider asked.

"I'd be pleased to meet them," Raymond answered.

The vet motioned the others over to Raymond's table.

"I'm Glen Olsson, and this is my wife, Fran," he said, placing an arm around her shoulder. "This here's Red Dixon, although he ain't as red as he used to be when we were in 'Nam. And this is Rebecca Gordon, his intended." He turned to his friends, sweeping a hand toward Raymond.

"Y'all, this is Ray Thornton, the guy who wrote the book. He's the reason we came down here."

Raymond rose and greeted them. Then he introduced everyone at the table.

"This is Bud Oswald. He is the county sheriff."

Bud stood, put down his napkin, and shook hands.

"Sheriff, I'm real pleased to meet you," said Rebecca. "We've kinda been having a little debate. If you don't mind me asking, how's the crime down here in God's country?"

Raymond smiled as he watched Bud cross his arms and tap his chin with two fingertips. Bud took his time to consider the question. After a long pause, he spoke.

"It's good," he said. "Real good."

While the visitors made their way back to their table, Raymond and his friends overheard Rebecca speaking to Red.

"See, Dix? That's what I been telling you. We should live in a place like this where nothing ever happens."

Wally used his fork to point over his shoulder.

"There's a lady over there with a good point too," he said.

Lucy thought about that for a moment. Then she turned to Bud and spoke.

220

"Good job Sheriff," she said. "Thank you."

"You're darn right," Raymond said.

He held up his coffee cup to acknowledge Bud.

"To the sheriff."

They all lifted their drinks in a toast.

"Not to me," Bud said, "but to those who are no longer with us."

The clinking of glasses went on for awhile.

CHAPTER FIFTY-TWO

First Letter To Millie

January 26, 1977

Dear Millie,

I underestimated the pain of losing you. I listen for the sound of your steps at the door, but they never come. I barge into the cabin to tell you what I just saw, but you are not here. This is the best I can do.

Yesterday morning, long before God woke up, the sky faded from black to cobalt blue. It took forever. I watched it. Snow covered everything with little marshmallow caps right down to the water's edge. Not a breath of wind stirred, and the surface of the lake looked like polished slate. Strands of fog danced on the water, waving scarves at the sky. It took an hour for the sunlight to creep down the hillside, cross the lake, and burn the dancers off the water.

I heard you calling me. I sat shivering in the Adirondack chair on the dock, nursing my scotch. It's what I do to kill the pain and stop the brain. Of course, nothing improves while I drink. I just survive. That's my sole objective now. I am no longer gung-ho to take that hill, hold this line, clear that tunnel. I just want to be alive in the morning in case there's an extraction. So, I watch through the night, ready to call in artillery and air support, and wait for an answer to the big question: why?

A mongrel showed up on the porch yesterday, gaunt, round-eyed, with a wizened old face that reveals every thought. He apologized for tracking snow up onto the porch, but it had frozen into clumps between his toes and pads. Although he has ribs like a radiator, he didn't beg. He just looked at me with those weary eyes, happy enough to curl up in a dry place. I took him in, fed him, and listened to his stories. We fell asleep in front of the fire, both of us hungry for the physical contact of another living thing. He has nice ears, and he uses them well. Today I told him about you. He wants to meet you. He thinks you are … just away. Me too.

My chest hurts. It feels like steel bands are wrapped around me, and someone tightens them a little each day. Yesterday my heart felt like it was going to explode. My pulse raced, heart pounding like a fist hitting me in the chest again and again, and I was so weak that I just sat in the snow. I was unable to breathe. So I drank. It's not the solution, I know. I stole my theme song from Pete Seeger.

If I can get hammered,
I'll get hammered in the morning,
I'll get hammered in the evening,
All over this land.
I'll get hammered over justice,
I'll get hammered over freedom,
I'll get hammered over love between my brother and my sister
All over this land.

Think I'll call the dog Extraction. Tracker for short. He showed up at the right time. Maybe he can get me out of here. I've got to go. I'm out of scotch. I'll write again, when I can hold two ideas together up to the sunlight. Meanwhile, just know that I am dead without you.

Love,

Raymond

LaVergne, TN USA
07 July 2010
188602LV00004B/5/P